DIVIDED

Published in the United Kingdom in 2020

Divided Publishing Ltd
Rue André Hennebicqstraat 43
1060 Brussels
Belgium

http://divided.online

Cover design by Salu
Book design by Luuse
Printed by Graphius Brussels

ISBN 978-1-9164250-2-6

Fanny Howe

NIGHT PHILOSOPHY

Seen no matter how and said as seen.

Lamb, you have fallen into milk.

Introduction

This book is made from torn parts. Prose broken by other prose, all of it written on the cusp of a long millennium.

During childhood I lived in an apartment near Boston that smelled like a wooden drawer. Very brick, very quiet, where natural life tapped the windowpanes and voices sang and barked and changed tones.

Each book was a physical model of time: words pressed together in darkness, then flipped open to light, then sealed again.

Mysterious sources shadowed every word and illustration. I held the book up to my face and breathed in. The fragrance was the nearest thing to nothing. Nothing being everything that wasn't visible or present to me at that moment.

History with its gray and metallic waves that rocked from shore to shore was the killer of this ethereal realm. I saw the pictures in the papers, the news that preceded the movies, so I could never see a way to prolong the pleasure of not knowing what was outside.

End-Song

During life I wanted to be buried in a mystery.
On a western estuary where seabirds nest.

To drop into a piece of muck and shell, unnamed.

Wind, low clouds, rain and shafts of sun. Monks, poets,
vapors of the deep.
Now where do I want to be buried?

Without an urn, there will be dirt that my ashes will disturb.
Why an urn at all?

Can't you burn into nothing?

Isn't the sky what I expected to become?
Does gravity hang on to bones like a registry of comings
and goings?

Where to be buried, where to be thrown: from what
mouth sing.

Once a Child

She referred to her own libido as an inverted worm, whirling like a screw into the source of her being.

She couldn't want anything less, or little enough.

The wolves in her forest were dressed in uniforms. Although she sported no yellow pigtails, no freckles, no lily-green skin, and not even the dirndl or the kilt and safety pin, she feared being an Aryan.

Freud would say her anxiety began at birth and then later with her steplike-mother, but existentialists would say it was "built in" to being in the world.

She said that she knew how it felt during the war, although she just missed the actual experience.

The doctor had a good generous face, bright honest eyes and a black beard.

Being extremely short, he bought his clothes in the boys' department and exuded the power of a man who must compensate hourly for his missing inches.

These lazy women who surrounded his days helped him stay sane.

He would muse: "They are the last heretics against a work-addicted world. In a post-industrial modern society, these mad women lounging around hospitals are the true defenders of a time on earth when work did not prove worth."

"How can you just loll around all day, doing nothing?" he asked her once.

She replied: "How can you just walk around all day, idly watching us?"

Both of them were forest-dwellers, after all, preferring the company of the wild to the tame.

But it was a long time before the doctor figured out a way to get her to function rationally, above all consistently, outside the hospital ward.

One day he offered her the job of gardener on the grounds around the hospital and told her he would set her up in a little cottage near the front gates and on a four-lane highway.

And as if trying to make her feel useful and intelligent, he asked her advice about his patients. She generalized: "The wholly wounded have to be wholly healed."

He thought she had said "holy" and his mind wandered nervously away.

Always he feared the return of her manias.

Now she grabbed his hands in hers and examined them with tears on her lashes, saying: "Your pink nails are like seashells, your knuckles are so brown . . . Why do they make me cry for joy?"

Backing away, he replied: "Calm down, it's nothing. My dear friend, since most of the world is absent, air should be your model of heaven. Not physical details."

And later that day he gave her a little excerpt from Kafka's notebooks that she pinned over her bed. He supposed that he played the part of God in her life, or maybe she even fantasized about loving him.

"Strange how the legacy of cynicism is belief," he reflected, thinking how her parents must have treated her.

And a week later he heard her begin her story where she always began: "One night many years ago—from under a dry rose bush—in a rough garden near the Irish Sea."

As soon as I was halfway through the story, I heard him breathing in low regular patterns and discovered to my amazement that I had put my doctor to sleep.

It was wonderful to gaze on his closed face, to see his hands folded on his chest mid-twiddle, thumbs upright, and his mouth ajar. His soft eyelids were flat against their orbs, he didn't seem to be dreaming. His will and his intellect had fled. His notebook dangled like a children's storybook from his parted knees.

A Useful Man

Jacques Lusseyran began his life story:

"As I remember it, my story always starts out like a fairy tale, not an unusual one, but still a fairy tale . . . I was born in 1924, on 19 September at noon, in the heart of Paris in Montmartre, between the Place Blanche and the Moulin Rouge. I was born in a modest nineteenth-century house, in a room looking out over a courtyard."

He had a loving middle-class childhood that made his days all right because of the safety his parents provided and because he knew he was happy. However, happiness and childhood were not to be his subject. It was, instead, the answer to someone's question: What are your reasons for loving life? Light.

"I saw it everywhere I went," he writes, "and watched it by the hour. None of the rooms in our three-room apartment has remained clear in my memory. But the balcony was different, because on the balcony there was light. Impetuous as I was, I used to lean patiently on the railing and watch the light flowing over the surfaces of the houses in front of me and through the tunnel of the street to right and left.

"This light was not like the flow of water, but something more fleeting and numberless, for its source was everywhere. I liked seeing that the light came from nowhere in particular, but was an element just like air . . . Radiance multiplied, reflected itself from one window to the next, from a fragment of wall to cloud above. It entered into me, became part of me. I was eating sun.

"This fascination did not stop when night fell. When I came in from outdoors in the evening, when supper was over, I found the fascination again in the dark. Darkness, for me, was still light, but in a new form and a new rhythm. It was light at a slower pace. In other words, nothing in the world, not even what I saw inside myself with closed eyelids, was outside this great miracle of light."

Then, at the age of eight, a minor accident at school rendered him totally blind. From that moment he saw no more the world he had just described to us. Instead he heard sounds he had never heard before; an avalanche of noises filled each room, and he felt people as colors that he could see interiorly. Like an alert bird, or a worm whose perceptions covered the whole of his body, he was able to hear that "sound has the same individuality as light."

He said: "My accident had thrown my head against the humming heart of things, and the heart never stopped beating." His parents, with transcendent calm, helped him continue where he left off. It is almost as if a supernatural force suddenly gave him and his parents an assignment that they never applied for; he had to be calm, blind, and articulate so that he could witness the history that was coming their way.

He mastered braille in six weeks and returned to school and his friends there. The family for a time lived in Toulouse, where he could freely wander in the countryside. Then they moved back to Paris, where he had a close friend named Jean with whom he did everything throughout his childhood and youth. In this friendship he developed into a social animal; there was unlimited trust exchanged in their hours spent together. The two made his blindness into an opportunity to discover the properties of the invisible. He shared all he learned with Jean and others and was followed by a parade of boys wherever he went.

The first thing he discovered, soon after his accident, was that there was a source of light that was not the sun; it hid within his body; he was flooded by it and because of it, he felt the presence of others and objects through their colors. The light in him responded to an aura of color. He could smell and taste colors and feel the shape and tone of a wall without touching it. People arrived dressed in the colors of their characters.

He never gave the light divine attributes. He did not embellish his description of it with religious language. It was not a symbol, not a myth, not magic for him. It wasn't a sign; it was as embodied as a spine. Blindness did not drive him insane, although blindness looks insane to others. People fear the blind the way their fear madness. But Lusseyran was not mad.

He lived at home in occupied Paris, passed his exams, and walked to his classes with his stick and his friends. He took philosophy, psychology, and history—the last being his favorite—while Marshal Pétain roared over the loudspeakers.

The French police began to imitate the Nazis. And he and his friends decided to form a resistance group made up of students.

The meetings took place in the Lusseyran family house on the boulevard de Port-Royal. They called themselves the Volunteers of Liberty and he was given the task of interviewing everyone who wanted to become a Volunteer. He took his time with each interview, feeling out the timbre of the personality, the stability of the background, the nuance of the personality in the room with him. The group mimeographed a bulletin and disseminated it throughout the city. They were described as terrorists. (Nearby, in her parents' apartment, Simone Weil was also writing and holding meetings.)

Though the French government denounced all such activities and paid informers to turn people in, Lusseyran kept at it. For him most importantly he planned to take the special exam to qualify for the École Normale Supérieure, but he soon learned that Nazi biomedical laws made students with disabilities ineligible. Deeply disappointed, Jacques became ever more involved with the Resistance and merged his group with a larger one, the Défense de la France. In 1942 the Nazis ordered all French men over twenty-one to be sent to Germany as forced laborers, and thousands went. The Défense de la France went deeper underground.

Then something else went terribly wrong. Lusseyran, still the one in charge of interviewing new recruits for the Défense, interviewed as a matter of course a man named Elio. During their time in the small room together, the light that usually suffused Lusseyran with the confidence to judge the quality of the person before him, failed.

He watched as something like a strip of darkness fell across his eyes, and he recoiled. Elio had a weak handshake and an unclear way of speaking. But Lusseyran let him join the Défense de la France because of his skills. Within a short time Elio had betrayed him and his friends to the Gestapo. Lusseyran was taken away and beaten but refused to name names or cooperate. And in July 1943 he was sent to Buchenwald.

Incarcerated for months and months and months, he experienced the world as he always had. There was no beginning or end to any sound, no matter how particular (a shout, a shot, a thump, a voice). They were indivisible, the way water and all its contents are. And that solid and steady light that intensified all his other senses enabled him to live an engaged life. He formed friendships, became a leader in the French Resistance inside the camps through translation and the transmission of overheard news reports in German to other prisoners. In January 1944, there were sixty thousand prisoners at Buchenwald. Six months later there were ten thousand. Lusseyran gives a full report on the months he lived there, and the people he knew and cared for, most of whom died.

"All through February," he writes, "they kept us in quarantine in crowded barracks removed from the active center of the camp. It was hard to bear because of the cold. In the dead center of Germany, near the edge of Saxony, and on the top of that high hill, fifteen hundred feet above the plain, the temperature fluctuated between five and twenty degrees below zero . . . I must be frank. The hardest thing was not the cold, not even that. It was the men themselves, our comrades and other prisoners, all the ones sharing out miseries. Suffering had turned some into beasts . . . worse than the beasts were the possessed. For years the SS had so calculated the terror that either it killed or it bewitched. Hundreds of men at Buchenwald were bewitched. The harm done them was so great that it had entered into them body and soul. And now it possessed them. They were no longer victims. They were doing injury in their turn and doing it methodically."

Near the end of his account, he tells his readers how to get through torture, through imprisonment. There are three things to remember: "The first of these is that joy does not come from outside for whatever happens to us it is within. The second truth is that light does not come to us from without. Light is in us, even if we have no eyes." The third is friendship. If you can form close human attachments to those around you, you have the possibility of surviving as a human being.

Originally typed on a braille typewriter, Lusseyran's story unfolds as a slowly developing film, the way the light spills over a city. His blindness (the ultimate loneliness) put him in touch with the source of being. There he dwelled in a state of potentiality, in a place that precedes the blast of creation.

The blind are dependent on passing strangers in a variety of situations. A man will stop and stand on rue Saint-Jacques with his red-tipped stick in his hand, and he will wait until a voice comes to him, offering help. Then he will allow himself to be steered through sheets of steel and engines to get to the other side of the street. He will assent. His body will not resist or expect. He will let himself be helped by a person he will never meet again; his loneliness has made availability to friendship indispensable.

Even though the Lusseyran story insists on the existence of an interior light that affirms another source than the sun, he confesses that there were times "when the light faded, almost to the point of disappearing. It happened every time I was afraid."

Night Class for Children

The poetics of a story is the narrative structure that holds it all together.

This structure includes relationships between people, creatures, nature and weather that interact with and affect each other.

The narrative structure reflects the way the storyteller reads the world: 1. as a social network with survival alone as its purpose; or 2. as a testing ground for a spiritual being who may or may not find happiness on earth.

The structure of the narrative is made out of the actions of those who can act, and those who can speak through dialogue. They act and speak on behalf of the storyteller and the idea behind the story.

The idea behind the structure is often a social convention, a moral lesson, a warning, an encouragement.

It is called "poetics" because it describes a structure that is so unified in all its parts that it is, like a science and a poem, a door into the whole (holistic) nature of life itself.

*

For lucky children, many of them boys, there is a classic sequence of actions that you find in legends, myths, folk and fairy stories.

The call to adventure, when you choose to leave home.

The hesitation when you turn back. And the impulsive decision to go forth.

Each one of those moments could make up a whole novel.

But soon you have to enter the larger world, and its mysteries and foreignness represented (as in Pinocchio) by a whale's belly.

And you struggle now, relying on the kindness of strangers, often women.

You reconcile yourself to being your father's child, and not a world-stranger.

People come to your help, especially those who recognize you.

You begin to notice a kind of magic to coincidental encounters and timing.

You take advantage of these, by putting your trust in their logic.

And you now can return home as someone who has familiarized the outside world.

*

Or this might happen:

You are banished from your home or kingdom because of some infraction of rules or mistake.

You are given overwhelming tasks, penalties.

You are defined according to your social class, gender and profession.

You are swept away by an evil (ogre, witch) being who makes animals seem like kin.

Pieces of good fortune give you temporary hope, and some secret gift that is yours alone, and that you can use.

You are enslaved.

Your temperament is often the cause of your survival, especially if you are humble, simple, can recognize wonder signs and the language of animals and nature. These "come to your rescue" because you let them. And you come to a safe place at last, usually one embedded in the natural world, nearly Paradise.

The individual is greater than the collective in the West. In parts of Asia it is alright to tell small lies if they serve the collective, but not if they are on your own behalf. The goal in both cases is a safe place, with abundant natural resources and beauty, and friends close by, and growing families.

Only by learning the complex nature of the outside world, and how to read its signs of hospitality and hostility are you able to find or build a safe society (home).

1994

My friend Marilyn Buck, American political prisoner, grew up in Texas where her father was an Episcopal minister who worked for civil rights. He was an activist who picketed and criticized the bishop; crosses were burned on his lawn and he was fired from his ministry. His actions, to his eldest daughter, were embarrassing and, later, inadequate.

Many daughters in those days wanted to serve their fathers by outdoing them in their political lives.

Hers was known as the Resistance Conspiracy Case. This group of four women helped Assata Shakur escape to Cuba. In 1967 Marilyn became actively involved in supporting Native Americans, Mexicans, Vietnamese, Palestinians, Iranians, Puerto Ricans and Black Americans in their liberation struggles. The RCC were anti-imperialist and socialist and the FBI had them, with thousands of others, on their lists.

Marilyn left Texas to join Students for a Democratic Society (SDS) in 1967. In 1973 the FBI accused her of being a member of the Black Liberation Army and she was sentenced to ten years in jail for buying two boxes of handgun ammunition that she never used. She was designated a "high security prisoner" and in 1977 she was granted a furlough from which she didn't return.

She was caught and imprisoned again and this time the charges were far more serious and she got eighty years in high security. During the 90s I visited her in prison where she wrote poetry and prose. She was not repentant (none of the four were) but very conscious of the difficulties of speaking truth.

She gave me some of her writing, which a tiny magazine called *Parenthesis* published.

This was one thing she said:

"I live with a peculiar kind of fear. Fear of getting so wrapped up in the contradiction of self-censorship that holding on to the essential inner truth and being becomes difficult. Fear of losing the ability to maintain my identity and humanity. How long can one stay conscious of each act of self-censorship before it becomes a habit no less potent than an alcohol or drug addiction?

"Where is that place within the self that enables one to resist—to carry on? Not to let the act of shielding the self from the invaders become the weapon of my own self-disintegration, bringing the directive to fruition; not to allow it to transform itself into cowardice and fear of the state; not to turn tail and run and run until one reaches the point at which one leaves behind that essential part of the self—that sense of humanity that demands, urges resistance, that part which has led so many of us to be revolutionaries and partisans of justice.

"The fear of succumbing to self-censorship as well as to the state's censorship is a real fear.

"It has happened to comrades who, through fear, or through 'maintaining a low profile,' ultimately lost their voices and became nothing more than whispers so low that not even they themselves could hear.

"We censor ourselves to survive. The rage at the violation of our lives is inexpressible. Each of us has to decide how to guard our interior beings, to protect our psyches from being profiled, analyzed and assailed. Every waking moment is a knowing moment. We cannot even sit down and have casual conversations about where we used to hang out, who our friends were, because there are prisoners who are encouraged, and believe it to be to their advantage, to inform the officials of what they hear, what they weave from innocuous, innocent words. Too many times such casual talk has ended up in FBI files.

"The watchers, those select few trained in the skills of psychological observation and analysis, who implement the 'special programs'—they know we understand. Do they wait to see if our efforts to survive and resist can withstand the daily pressure of the watching, the censoring? Do they think our efforts to guard our identities will entrap us and our own self-censoring will, in the end, serve the directive?"

Indivisible

I locked my husband in a closet one fine winter morning. It was not a large modern closet, but a little stuffy one in a century-old brick building. Inside that space with him were two pairs of shoes, a warm coat, a chamber pot, a bottle of water, peanut butter and a box of crackers. The lock was strong but the keyhole was the kind you can both peek through and pick. We had already looked simultaneously, our eyes darkening to the point of blindness as they fastened on each other, separated by only two inches of wood. Now I would not want to try peeking again. My eyes meeting his eyes was more disturbing than the naked encounter of our two whole faces in the light of day. It reminded me that no one knew what I had done except for the person I had done it with. And you God.

Shut Up

Now the millennium has come and gone, and I am in a hermitage facing a field of snow and bristling grain where there is a line of gray trees at the end. The sky has the wintry golden blush that makes it seem to swell like water. I hear cars and trucks in the distance. Over the years I have written during days just like these, when there was snow, or cold, and some sense of safety and enclosure. More often I have written on the road in the middle of children, crowds at train stations, airports, motels, bus depots, in offices and schoolyards.

I have put this collection on the table in order to discover what I was doing during those times, because it was not just a matter of writing experience. That activity was inseparable from the dialectical questions of my generation, from the paradoxes of a life spent in a cynical social terrain. America.

Why was I chained to these problems that I myself had created? Why all this scratching and erasing? It was more like drawing an invisible figure than painting what was in front of me. I wanted something to recognize: a disembodied presence. I could only find it by discovering a just system in syntax.

A friend wrote down some words for me shortly before he died: "Poetry is backwards logic. You can't write poetry unless you have knowledge of, or taste for, this 'backwards' way of finding truth."

Another person said sound is eternal, it has no beginning. And a Hindu teacher said to me, "The Upanishads were never written for the first time."

Years ago I walked into a café in Los Angeles to meet a poet I had never met or spoken to before (Gustaf Sobin). I was carrying Plotinus, for company in case he wasn't there, and he was at the bar, reading Plotinus.

To be truly open you don't need dogma or a pen.
You are either facing the endless open or you are letting it face you.

A coincidence is perfect, intimate attunement.

There was an Irish philosopher in the ninth century who wrote about God and the world in a way I could recognize. Eriugena was his name. He said this through translation, so it may be wrong:

"The speed at which God moves is what establishes the impassable distance between what one sees and what is seen. God is always running and crossing God 'to join the two ends' of itself, by being already within itself. It remains contained even while it is speeding. Humanity is always dropping out of the race out of despair; one's voice calls out to announce one's existence by sound and visibility that can't occur without a witness.

"How could I say that the experience of God now is as appearance in music and coincidence, dreams and disappearance. It convenes and amasses, it dissolves and passes. One only senses it. The miracle of the eye makes the philosophy of light essential. The eye organizes but is it seeing? It sees what it saw before. The violet on the stem."

This is an effort to resolve the question: what was this strange preoccupation that seemed to have no motive, cause, or final goal and preceded all that writing that I did. Did it begin in the environment of childhood, or was it formed out of alien properties later? If I had known what I was doing all along, would I have done it? What guided me? What could I call what I was calling?

Dear Master:

The air is too clear in America: sharp are the figures approaching like digitized images on a flat screen. The clouds are way high up. Humans are like pressed thorns and flowers on a wall. The faces burst with appetite and pride. Bicycles whir past at a violent pace with commercials pasted on the backs of the bikers. They seem to be more chemical than biological, the whites with their teeth and ambitions, already robotic, beyond science fiction even, and back on this earth radiating the poisons they have manufactured and used and become.

When I am at home all street sound bounces between the buildings facing it. Five stories up, I can hear the whisper of a child below, but I can't see the whisper and have to lean way out to see the child. There are men and women in uniforms.

They came into my apartment armed with warrants. Red light, two cars, deep-blue flashes. It was dazzling. Most guards like angels keep such a low profile, you walk through them. They turn away from your weaker moments and prefer not to see what is happening. This was NOT one of those occasions. I felt that heaven was very close to earth and there was no space between here and the afterlife. All judgment was attached to recognition.

But there was NO WAY OUT of anywhere.

*

Sometimes the syntax of poetry helps me to see what life is really doing, and to find the key to the open air.

J.M. Coetzee said Hölderlin had "the habit of breaking open a perfectly good poem, not in order to improve it, but to improve it from the ground up. In such a case, which is the definitive text, and which the variant, particularly when the rebuilding is broken off and not resumed?"

When I was writing poems: the words I heard, my thoughts, that is, formed a single unit of sound, and then another, that I wanted to transcribe fast. I wanted to keep the sense of the first thought alive, by replicating the sounds exactly or echoing them. So I would scrawl them all over the place as fast as I could, by hand, and then come back to the fragments and try to organize them as if they were spoken or a letter to someone and I knew what I was saying.

Recognition of a face and language is the only reassurance I have of my sanity. Still, I have tried to recognize the missing figure behind the poem as it fled from one idea to another.

Is a thing recognized because its first appearance lives as a god? Or is it only what you have gotten used to.

Hölderlin: "Human beings can carry the divine only sometimes."

In 1800 Hölderlin embarked on an exhausting translation of Pindar's lyric poetry from Greek into German and in the process created "the true language of elsewhere," something strange and distant. He used that tone and grammar for his poetry thereafter. I wonder whose translation captures that foreign tone the best. Would it be the first translator? The closest to the time of Hölderlin? Or the most recent?

This is my prose translation of "Bread and Wine" by Hölderlin:

We've come too late to know what the gods were, only that they live in another sphere, way off in the universe now, passing sometimes like the sound of thunder. We might at night receive guidance from them in our dreams. But we humans rarely contain them for long. We exist in solitude so the night fills us with fear. We long for sleep. Even more than friends! So what good are poets in times like these? Wine-drinkers, lonely wanderers, philosophers of the night.

Childhood War
by Ilona Karmel,
1945

This story begins like any other.
A childhood story as ordinary
As milk and flowers. A world so small
That it could be contained within four walls.

The tale begins in an aura of tenderness
And calm though also in a world
So huge that Mother's
Hands had to protect us.

There was a children's room
With blue walls and ceilings
And when the day broke open
Outside the window the sky
Merged with our ceiling

And everything then was golden blue.
That day—my God—was short.

We couldn't fathom all its wonders
Before the light began to fade
And the sun disappeared. The lamp
Flickered sleepily, darkness trailed

From its hiding places out in the town.
It glued itself to our windows—
It was stifling—and we tossed.

And then that darkness became something else.

Whispers, rustles, chatters
From a primeval woodland
Joined the silver patterns on the wallpaper
And became forty thieves.

Number 16 Dluga Street is still there,
I am sure, crammed in
Between the same houses
That were standing when I was a child.

In the park the maples bloom and droop.
But childhood is gone
Fast and for good, who can say
Where it went? The world around

Shriveled up and grew small.
I don't know how. Now
Nothing is mysterious.
Nothing survived the pogrom

Not the elves
Sprites, gnomes, or little folk.
They were not saved
Any more than the secrets in the drawers.

The fantasies fell slowly, heavily
And brutally.

The tub is no longer an ocean,
The whale nothing to fear

And the chestnut is just a chestnut.
What is good fortune, I ask . . .

Now fear doesn't lurk in the dusk.
Darkness is tempting instead.
The dangerous unknown
Looks good. A mother is superfluous.

Farewell, childhood! Hello, youth!
A splendid, gigantic
World of stories and adventures
When we still counted the years.

And before a new way of computing
Time began—by days, hours, fears.
We measured time when I was fourteen.
No words to explain.

The Plant

Years ago but not many, two teens, Ilona and her sister Henia, were sent from Płaszów to a forced labor camp in central Poland. HASAG in Skarżysko-Kamienna was a factory taking advantage of the war economy and there they faced monotonous machine work, typhus, hunger, overcrowding. The camp was divided into Werk sections A, B and C. The Karmels wound up in C, the worst. Here prisoners were turned into objects if they did anything out of place—they were painted different colors and wrapped in paper sacks, walking skeletons put out to strike horror into the hearts of other prisoners.

The first two camps were primarily devoted to ammunition, and the third, Werk C, to the production of underwater mines filled with picric acid. Prisoners turned yellow and died from this horrific work. The factories had two twelve-hour shifts. Selection occurred randomly when any prisoner might be shot by a troop of factory police. Jewish prisoners had to haul the bodies of other prisoners to a mass grave. Only when there began to be a critical shortage of factory workers did the conditions there improve at all.

There was continual resistance from inside the barbed wires, and it was here that many poems similar to this one were written. A non-Jewish worker in the plant gave Henia and Ilona extra worksheets to write on. These sheets were handed in to the boss at the end of every day, but one side was blank. It was on these blank worksheets that the poems were composed in pencil (also very difficult to get hold of) and then concealed.

After their liberation from Buchenwald in 1945 they wrote this statement about their poems:

"We look at them in astonishment, powerless before their strangeness. It's as if we were meeting old friends after years of separation. They are known, but foreign because of an impassible chasm—time and distance. Words spat out in a fever, screamed poems, now sound like weak whispers, almost inaudible. Experiences, which we tried to reproduce in all their horrible reality, have slipped into pallid outlines, already almost erased.

"When we look at them, before our eyes we see inscriptions upon the walls of prisons and camps, scrawled at the last moment by people who have already passed on. Cries for help, calls for revenge, an unfinished sentence terminated mid-point, maybe only a name and a date, the terror of those days marked clumsily by a weakening hand upon a hard, indifferent wall. Today only half-readable traces stay on the wall.

"These poems are exactly that: inscriptions on a prison wall. They are feeble efforts to preserve a record. Why make such an effort to leave behind a trace, and to transmit one's experience before it is all over? What forced us to do this?

Was it the pain or was it a protest against the absolute end of things?

"No. Having been taught by machine guns to think in categories of thousands and millions, we had reconciled ourselves to the unimportance of the individual. So did we write in order to transmit the information and thereby incite people later to vengeance? No. In those days we understood the complete futility of trying to match any punishment to this crime."

The Rights of the Child (UN) Known Only to Adults

The child shall enjoy all the rights set forth in this Declaration. Every child, without any exception whatsoever, shall be entitled to these rights, without distinction or discrimination on account of race, color, sex, language, religion, political or other opinion, national or social origin, property, birth or other status, whether of himself or of his family.

The child shall enjoy special protection, and shall be given opportunities and facilities, by law and by other means, to enable him to develop physically, mentally, morally, spiritually and socially in a healthy and normal manner and in conditions of freedom and dignity. In the enactment of laws for this purpose, the best interests of the child shall be the paramount consideration.

The child shall be entitled from birth to a name and a nationality.

The child shall enjoy the benefits of social security. He shall be entitled to grow and develop in health; to this end, special care and protection shall be provided both to him and to his mother, including adequate pre-natal and post-natal care.

The child shall have the right to adequate nutrition, housing, recreation and medical services.

The child who is physically, mentally or socially handicapped shall be given the special treatment, education and care required by his particular condition.

The child, for the full and harmonious development of his personality, needs love and understanding. He shall, wherever possible, grow up in the care and under the responsibility of his parents, and, in any case, in an atmosphere of affection and of moral and material security; a child of tender years shall not, save in exceptional circumstances, be separated from his mother. Society and the public authorities shall have the duty to extend particular care to children without a family and to those without adequate means of support. Payment of State and other assistance towards the maintenance of children of large families is desirable.

The child is entitled to receive education, which shall be free and compulsory, at least in the elementary stages. He shall be given an education which will promote his general culture and enable him, on a basis of equal opportunity, to develop his abilities, his individual judgement, and his sense of moral and social responsibility, and to become a useful member of society.

The best interests of the child shall be the guiding principle of those responsible for his education and guidance; that responsibility lies in the first place with his parents.

The child shall have full opportunity for play and recreation, which should be directed to the same purposes as education;

society and the public authorities shall endeavor to promote the enjoyment of this right.

The child shall in all circumstances be among the first to receive protection and relief.

The child shall be protected against all forms of neglect, cruelty and exploitation. He shall not be the subject of traffic, in any form.

The child shall not be admitted to employment before an appropriate minimum age; he shall in no case be caused or permitted to engage in any occupation or employment which would prejudice his health or education, or interfere with his physical, mental or moral development.

The child shall be protected from practices which may foster racial, religious and any other form of discrimination. He shall be brought up in a spirit of understanding, tolerance, friendship among peoples, peace and universal brotherhood, and in full consciousness that his energy and talents should be devoted to the service of his fellow men.

Cut

A poem picked me up at 11 from drive across Ireland—3 hours, it filled me in while mist dripped over everything outside. As ever startling + breakthrough things to me—about "church is dead." A virtual community of Johannine believers. The spirit moving it all in + thru odd places. The movability, coming from everywhere, to be open + to assent

Exitus et reditus

↑

Aquinas kind of thought
God dealing with God—
The leaving of Mass to find the Poem.

Rhododendrons in full wet _____? Splendor yellow grouse in bloom. Clouds lying on ground.

June 8

June 9

Walked last night up with the poem thru the seventeenth-century gardens—lavender + herbs + roses, then a Bible garden of all herbs mentioned, fruit trees pinned to the walls, red Chinese lanterns, an orchard outside—apples, plums, pears—pressed into juice (service)—the view to the Galtee Mountains—behind there was a steep path through a ferny, green bower muddy path—a brook beside—enchanted—up steps + over + down. Now the poem is gone.

The Rose

In a monastery garden, each brook is dry, even the fountain. Terracotta, mariposa, roses, tourists and sweet Orthodox incense—are linked by the parching air.

It's quiet, until a woman covers her mouth of laughs. The Bishop is laughing, now, too, at his own joke: that an asp is both a poison, and a snake! The shadow of a sound turns around a stone sundial, though we can't see its motion: as if to prove the intention is the shaper of result, regardless of attention.

I had driven both length and breadth, looking for a way to love again. But my breath broke down where the hills spread out like bread and pies on a bakery shelf. The immensity of production was overwhelming. Horizons in every direction.

Meanwhile there was this feast, not unlike a picnic or symposium, on a Sunday out of doors, with a crowd of us, not doing too much of this or that. Temperance came easy to some, under the tropical trees, but not to me. Temptation hovered, as it always does, where there's more than one person gathered, at the margins of our mouths, though each mind was focused on the discussion at hand.

"See," one said, "our own ideas, the fruit of our mind and the highest inspirations, were of no value without practice. Knowing what you know knowing to be (to being) you must judge others by a history, not a hope, but judge yourself conversely."

A thick-set rose dangled at a ninety-degree angle off a shrub overlooking a thin branch of water. It was one of those so red, it's nearly black, and fiercely scented. Like a certain brand of Czech wine, popular that summer, the rose was too thick for its own good, and before the petals had a chance to express their individuality, the whole clump fell on the checkered cloth.

*

We all were not really friends, of which there are so few, it's true all along what I once heard. With each disagreement came the recognition of our separation. It was all in a summer afternoon, dull in a way, only mildly distracting, empty of a customary will to power, until the subject of religious love arose.

Catholic

1.

What can you do after Easter?

Every turn of the tire is a still point on the freeway.

If you stand in one, and notice what is all around you, it is a pile-up of the permanent.

The churn of creation is a constant upward and downward action; simultaneous, eternal.

If you keep thinking there is only an ahead and a behind, you are missing the side-to-side which gives evidence to the lie that you are moving progressively.

If everything is moving at the same time, nothing is moving at all.

Time is more like a failed resurrection than a measure of passage.

2.

The drive from the I-5 along Melrose to Sycamore.

The drive up La Brea to Franklin and right then left up to Mulholland.

The drive along Santa Monica to the rise up to the right and Sunset.

The drive along Sunset east past the billboard of the man on a saddle.

The drive from the 405 up onto La Cienega and the view of hills. The difference between nirvana and nihil.

3.

Thomas Aquinas was an itinerant thinker. His thinking rolled like a reel.

It went forwards as a movement backwards. His thoughts may have been placed on the side like the eyes of many intelligent animals.

To mitigate pain he recommended weeping, condolence by friends, bathing, sleep, and contemplation of the truth.

He was the ninth of nine children and was sent very early to a monastery. The Dominicans luckily had no rule about staying in one place. So he could walk from city to city in Italy.

4.

Legal thoughts were developed by the Dominicans when they were assigned the job of creating penitential acts that matched each sin. They had to study humanity closely and seriously. Thomas took on this task as it became his life-work, his *Summa*, his body of words that he called straw in the end. Something to burn.

5.

Human nature: what is it?

The source and the destiny of each life are the same: an unknown that is unknowable. Unknown before; around and unknown now;

and unknown after unless already fully known before.

Every act and thought has to be measured against this that has no limits. Why?

Because the failure to grow and flourish and develop is a terror; to die prematurely without having found any consolation for disappointment is an injustice.
A person wants to be known, to add up, to be necessary.
The only way to assure that this can happen is for there to be a way to study each action in relation to its immediate objective and to its surrounding circumstance: who, what, where, by what ends, why, how, when. You can by these terms measure your action in the world, but its final objective remains the same: unknown.

6.

For some persons, meditation, contemplation, prayer indicate that there is an emptiness already built into each body and it is that which (paradoxically) makes them feel at home in the cosmos.

7.

For others the hoarding of capital signals a loss of desire for any more knowing; it substitutes number skips for information. It creates a safety net out of figures.

8.

The taste and smell of an action, any action, comes from its objective. This is the strange thing about relationship. What you desire is what creates your quality. You are not made by yourself, but by the thing that you want. It is that sense of a mutually seductive world that an itinerant life provides. Because you are always watching and entering, your interest in fixtures grows weary and your strongest tie is to the stuff off to the side traveling with you.

9.

Lemon-water light of California. Flattened with big boulevards and wandering men and women depleted at bus stops. Back-alley bungalows. A terry-cloth sash, evidence of neglect.

10.

The walk up Sycamore at night with Tom, looking in lighted windows and at varied architectures, Mediterranean and Mexican. The warm night's pungent gas-fume and flower.
Nights alone on Sycamore, grown children gone, windows open, bars and screens, my silver screen darting images onto my shirt.

The drive down La Brea at dawn to get onto the San Diego freeway with trucks and commuters catching the stock market opening in NYC. The lineaments of daybreak are silken tar and stars. Traffic is already on hard and Boston early-morning news.

11.

Passions are eliminations, but they are critical to the body's survival, because they attract, command, and absorb; they make vigilant. Hope and fear, these are the two passions that loom behind all the others. I know a man driven by fear, and another one deluded by hope.

12.

Pain interferes with your ability to concentrate. A priest told me to prepare for the end while I am still mentally ordered. Old age can scatter the work of a lifetime. Probably people should go *Sannyasa* as soon as they retire, and become wanderers, contemplatives, ones who act charitably all the day long.

13.

An ethics of intentionality must stay at a practical, measurable level, and never become abstract. Don't ever argue principles, my father told me. Stay with the facts.

14.

These scribbles? Stray ends? Ardor's droppings?
Illness has its own aura. And one who adores haloes can smell and see the aura of illness.
A thick swimmer. Through the door, an odor.
A mystifying sniff. Millions of them, worldwide.
Geese are going over, raw as a jet stream, the windows open and a stick finger plunged into a science jar. Seedless.

Nature exists in a deep sleep, Eden's sleep. This is why watching and hearing the wind in the trees or the waves brings such peace. If Natural Light is the imprint of Divine Light, the word Divine is unnecessary.

15.

In some form or other, the deformity of the form is always potential as opposed to immanent. Perfection requires attention.

16.

Asshole or jerk? Which one gets to be president.

You know the man by the punishment he deserves and doesn't get.
He can actually perfect his sin with malicious intent and no one will even notice. Because we have an infinite disposition for wanting the good.

17.

The freeway passes the airport and its glut of traffic, the planes' bellies ballooning over the lines of cars. Bullets and bombs and parachutes ghost and worm their way out of them to cover the head.
South lies ahead and more south, an opening to the sky bending down like the head of a lamb. I like the look of the mountain.
Mine eyes see the sun rising from mine east, they often have tears in them that will soon be blinding and blessing at the same time.
Long Beach and oil and electricity and the military built all the way to the beach—their forms the forms of insects who are empty of sleep.

Hills and fields around Irvine and the Lagunas. Fieldworkers bent over green and white. Now is the time for the Sixth International Brigade.

As I get older I don't remember what things are, only what they look like and are named. The way Los Angeles becomes hell at night after being purgatorial all day.
When allegory enters time, it is the sign of profound danger.

18.

The Dominicans, a young order, were given the task of instructing others in penances. Therefore, the study of human nature was critical. They soon found out that studying human action was the same as studying God and creation. Aquinas went on to discover that all labor is study of the divine since the divine is everything, and anyone who lives is stuck inside the structure of God the Cosmos. He was concerned with being, not doing. And his love for the world was so intense, it infused his thought with compassion for all things. He has been compared to Confucius, Sankara, phenomenology. He makes it possible for some people now to remain Catholic despite enormous misgivings and consciousness of the Church's bad acts. He's not the only one who makes it possible, but he is an important one because he is still considered an Angelic Doctor of the Church, one whose thought remains foundational in Catholicism. You can find his mind there, waiting, permitting, guiding right into modern-day life. He saw each person as an important piece of a magnificent puzzle made by and for God.

Plummet into that mystery if you want to know more.

19.

Aquinas walked until he banged into a tree, and then he collapsed and died soon after. He didn't want to write another line anyway. Modest and bewildered until the end. He never stopped equating joy with truth.

20.

I can't believe I can see. I can't believe I can hear. I can't believe I can speak or think. What are commodities but evidence of lost people. You cannot love a bathrobe so what can you love about your own texture.

21.

The airplanes' bellies and bonnets loom over the freeway landing at LAX. Ahead is south of south, Irvine, an opening to distance. I like the look of a mountain of matter.

22.

The hills plunge down to the Pacific that I forgot to view. Six a.m. en route to work. Deepening as the sun warms and lifts. Rev and veer and avoid exits at all costs. Rows of settlements will deteriorate, designed to fall lightly flat in an earthquake.

23.

Every turn of the tire stops at a halfway point to nothing. Parmenides. To walk this walk would be better, to walk from Sycamore Street to La Jolla.

One hundred miles.

The only end sought for in itself is the last end. It is always present in us, after, after. The sky all around.

The completion of ourselves.

24.

Evil is the privation of good in any subject, it is a weakness and a lack. This is why it is compatible with capital.

It may lack reason, or heart, or conscience, or empathy, it is a sign of incompletion, it is an exaggeration of one quality at the expense of others that must be banished in order for that one to thrive.

Intention is hardly distinguishable from morality. It colors the action that comes from it with the shade of the desired end. The sad thing is that you can apprehend your goal as good and be wrong. Most of the time this is what happens and so you have the problem of judging yourself in terms of both intention and desired end, when things go wrong.

25.

Where did I go wrong? At the same place everyone else did?

Why did I end up living in unhappiness for so many years?

Unhappiness was the desert, literally and figuratively.

Trees that don't move. Sun on dry dog turds. Black immobile shadows, temporary infinity.

This was not home because my interior landscape was composed of wet, watery images—soggy brick, flowerpots, begonias, big morning glories, sloppy roads, and turbulent skies. But something worse, generally, was occurring in the world around me, as it also occurred to me. The restless-ness, the consciousness of a disappearing base and goal, the lack of home and civic engagement. I loved no city that I recognized.

Anything can happen under these conditions. Nuclear bombs, dirty bombs, small-time random murder and abduction.

26.

At the Marine training base, the second border of Mexico begins, call it San Diego County. The twin-breasted nuclear power plant beside the pap-white sea. America stops here.

America is not located in the small beads of sand, the pelicans, dolphins, or the arching erotic hills. Fish tacos and a woman driving alone at dawn with immigrants packed inside the truck ahead of her.

We have left America to the conceptual capitalists.

But so-called Americans have settled here, as on the West Bank of Israel where cheap housing for U.S. Christians is expanding.

27.

A train runs parallel to its tracks and the freeway.

Eucalyptus borders the road through Leucadia along the tracks, heading south, the lettuce melting in the boxcars like a poor film sequence.

The second border on the other side of the freeway crossing north at the Marine training base. Ugly nuclear power plants, the humping hills.

Women running alone at dawn, aliens sending money home, in their wallets pictures of family and friends, love letters, addresses, I don't want to be here.

The canyons are groomed and pocked with bourgeois hous-
ing developments that are built for eclipse. The spirit mus-
cles its way out of disappointment and follows the body
laughing. Jesus after Easter is laughing all the way down
the road.

Tramps, boxcars, Marx, tacos, Dos Equis, rabbits uprooted
and fobbed onto parks, coyotes splitting into lonely wander-
ers, tractors, tanks, and brutalist walls. "This is the future,"
said a professor. The ocean forms a raised screen at the
end of every west-side road. Strange how it lifts like that.
Mustard carpeting the canyons.

28.

Night drive along Mission Boulevard, left on Turquoise
to get to the 5 South. Happy stop-offs, proximate ends,
promised lands, ruthless and armed RVs beside chugging
little geezers. Old Town to exit on Washington and up daz-
zled adobe trash to see the east out of a plate-glass window
on George, then back to Normal Street for chicken.

I am west or something. I don't know, but night clouds roll
out of the east as voluminous pitch that erases the stars.
I love being awake, someone said of her insomnia. She hid
the night in her closets and left the rest in color.

So nature remains but grace passes like a panopticon flowing
its light onto others in its slow circular motion.
Fugitive soul of the battered woman. She keeps running in
search of a safe-shaped geography. It could be as flat as the
desert. You are obliged to follow your reason, even helter-
skelter through the canyons. You are obliged because

there is inside you a living soul that fears annihilation before happiness can discover it.

29.

If something you do is good for more people than you yourself, you can be pretty sure it is the right thing. (That is, it will make you happy.)
Speed, aptitude, certitude. Direct yourself towards action. It is imperative to find a virtue in itinerancy because this is the world now. People are either fugitives who want to go home, or seekers who don't want to go home. The movement of immigrants across borders brings much suicide with it. Imperiled people give birth to more children than people who are settled and comfortable. The success of rabbits.
Sorrow weighs down your brain with water.

30.

All hope depends on possibility. But you can't have hope outside of an immediate, active concern for justice; and this complicates the processes.

Aquinas set out to prove that what we seek is actually what we are already.
This thought requires more thought. Another way of putting it is: when Aquinas equates God with happiness, we know what he means by happiness.

31.

The Egyptian women lied in order to protect the babies of the Hebrew women. God rewarded them for their lie. He gave them houses on earth. Moral ethicists are disturbed by this hypocrisy on God's part. But this is one way the notion of "person" is born. How is it lost?

32.

The intellect is contemplative.
Voluntary ignorance is a terrible social sin.
The embrace between faraway, freeway, and very near is air, breath, oil, here.
Mouth and food. Going somewhere you don't want to be. How does the will work. I don't want to go where I am going!
Peripatetic effusions.

33.

I pretend I trust surface truths, that I am moving forward, street by street, and everything I pass, is passed. I have a goal, a plan, and I receive what comes to me in the form of smell, sight, touch, sound.
The street that I can't see exists now in a state that will receive me as I enter it and everyone else will enter the next moment at the same moment I do. The world is round and I am walking it.
Time is space.
I pretend that I can take a step, with D—th directing traffic and earthquake and heartbeat and hate, is all I know of faith.

Doubt allows God to live.

34.

Sometimes you are privileged with a glimpse of the other world, when the light shines up from the west as the sun sets and dazzles something wet. The world is just water and light, a slide show through which your spirit glides.

Reason is the dominant weapon of oppression. (Reason vs. Person.)
Reason without the other values becomes evil.
Reason where it just lodges in me as an anonymous individual is still oppressive but it works best in harmony with other passions—people are depending on me, is the main one.

But if I were president, I would reason the world into horrific war because I would not let myself feel compassion or hope. I would eliminate passions that contradicted my reason.

35.

Plato believed that criminals wanted punishment. In a sense they committed the crime in order to suffer for having thought up evil in the first place. The crime was the proof of a worse evil: the mental plan. The crime allowed them to be punished for an intention.

In the same sense Aquinas knew that thought was contaminated, but he took circumstances into account and was not a judgmental kind of man, but he didn't have much truck with morose delectation, that kind of morbid indulgence in painful thoughts. Why, because they really undermine hope.

36.

I once spent a night near Massachusetts Bay, near Boston, Quincy graveyard, and home. I don't know why I agreed to this, because it was something I didn't want to do. I felt sorry for the person who asked me, and no wonder. She was a tramp with severe medical problems. She had been given a couch to sleep on for one night and wanted me to sleep on a thin bed upstairs. She didn't care about me. Now I realize that I did it because I wanted to know where the ground of being weakens.

I think you can know more if you do things that are fearful or unpleasant, as long as they do not include hospitals or jails.

Wanting to know is what makes me do things I don't want to do.
Wanting to know how far I can go with what I know.

37.

This is why I keep moving and only stop for the Eucharist in a church where there are sick, vomiting, maimed, screaming, destroyed, violent, useless, happy, pious, fraudulent, hypocritical, lying, thieving, hating, drunk, rich, poverty-stricken people.

Tar Pits

She laughed: "One is my lucky number!" Her sneakers were wearing down to two gnarled scoops, but she was never surprised that the vertical pronoun was also a number. On the apophatic path you choose to stay at the edge of the central city where you get a quasi-this and a quasi-that. In the diplomatic world transparency means non-ideological, neutral. In the walking world, it means eternal, invisible. One day clouds muffin against a tinny sky. L.A.'s a dirt heap, really, stuck with green nettles. A better shape to live in than the slabbish city. Cold and square as Forest Lawn. Why put a cake on a plate before putting it in your mouth? Why use a napkin instead of a sleeve to wipe away the dribble? I mean when I was walking the streets, she couldn't conceive of her own loneliness. Captain-bass-playing melodies got to it, though, a black sax, like a footbridge over cognac. New York is a whole deal. Yoni, sacred as a red anarchist, was given to every woman. Even the stepsister could say it twice. And her stepsister would say, exactly the way she would, "My stepsister hoped I would die." B-minus was her score. She began by a drink or three to keep her moving down lubricated avenues. There the faces of brown-skinned boys presented her with the problem of beauty. Africa refused to leave them alone in America. For this great act of mercy she was happy: for them there would be no erasure! Their beauty was a promise that couldn't be broken, it was Adam getting Even, it was as basic as a billy club. Let the academics sneer at the Jesuits, and go on being the hypocritical clerics of the century, she at least dared to believe in retribution. While one derelict liked malt, barley, and high altitudes, most of the others like herself preferred a cloud of mimosa breaking down the chicken-wire and feet firmly planted on the names of the stars embossed in Hollywood Boulevard. She had her private "names for the days of the weak"—Man Day, Dues Day, Wine Day, Thirst Day, Fried Day, Sat-Around Day, and the Sabbath. These were written in the earth-ball under her body's weight, where she was pleased to keep them.

A trough inside the Pacific Ocean led to an onshore flow. Then high seas, large swells, and a small-craft advisory. One storm system was weaker than the one before, and so did nothing to shift around the ozone, carbon monoxide, nitrogen dioxide, or the premenstrual syndrome in women's bodies. From the Southland mountains into the Valley, clouds pumped out shadows and rainbows. Palm leaves played on invisible keys, and the only children on the streets of Hollywood were lost children. Just as jazz makes white wine chill on a balcony, so stockings make syringes look like silver and nostril-rings resemble Disney tattoos. Shelter couches have rough skins and are not welcoming. Leather gloves, rip-hemmed jeans, sneakers, and Benadryl, all for sale. Kiss my casket, said one of nine thousand inmates. Two thousand have been given antibiotics against an outbreak of meningitis. One individual lay on a mattress in an unlighted cell, listening. It had to be a detour he was experiencing. He had hoped for notoriety when the means of his survival was found in obscurity. When he had begun performing actions that he knew were expected of him, he had already begun to lose his way. Now protected by darkness that his interior met with lighted, colorized dream stories, he could live without gas or refrigeration. He had come to this condition without even making a choice. It was rather as if someone had stuck up a sign in a lonely highway, and he had obeyed it, although it turned out to have been a joke intended for someone else to laugh about.

Soon she headed into the wind. Sepulveda Boulevard would lead her to the cornfields and crows of Scripture, a field gullied by rainfall, and parking lots where men sat in cars smoking. Sometimes they got out of their cars and went to the bathroom in a cement barrack. This action scared her back to creation. Rows of electric lights burned white in the daylight under a plastic tent. A model airplane buzzed across the field, but she was forbidden entrance to that nature preserve because she walked with a dog. Encircled by mountains, the Valley was a catcher for fog. Early mist dreamed over the dam. Brittle twigs screened her vista. Berries bled blue but were gray with dew, too. Two bodies had lain in mud the night before as she bolted across the San Diego Freeway. Yellow canvas covered them and she flinched to avoid a blue raindrop heading for her eye. Police lights were on the way. She had noticed earlier that angels, like mourning doves, coo to a Pyrrhic meter. Later she would take the square bread soaked in wine from an Eastern Orthodox priest and pray for those bodies. But that night she continued on past the end of their lives to the recycling center with her daily bag of cans.

Coyote scruff in canyons off Mulholland Drive. Fragrance of sage and rosemary, now it's spring. At night the mockingbirds ring their warnings of cats coming across the neighborhoods. Like castanets in the palms of a dancer, the palm trees clack. The HOLLYWOOD sign has a white skin of fog across it where erotic canyons hump, moisten, slide, dry up, swell, and shift. They appear impatient—to make such powerful contact with pleasure that they will toss back the entire cover of earth. She walks for days around brown trails, threading sometimes under the low branches of bay and acacia. Bitter flowers will catch her eye: pink and thin honeysuckle, or "mock orange." They coat the branches like lace in the back of a mystical store. Other deviant men and women live at the base of these canyons, closer to the city however. Her mouth is often dry, her chest tight, but she is filled to the brim with excess idolatry. It was like a flat mouse—the whole of Los Angeles she could hold in the circle formed by her thumb and forefinger. Tires were planted to stop the flow of mud at her feet. But she could see all the way to Long Beach through a tunnel made in her fist. Her quest for the perfect place was only a symptom of the same infection that was out there, a mild one, but a symptom nonetheless.

The Mohawk Special shovels up the lace of an elephant's
ear. (That's what the frozen ground is like.)
This is the year when half of my desire for you is the half
of yours for someone else.
It's the time when the working class means the unemployed.
The girl with the mandolin plays her catgut strings—for all
of us—until the trees outside are singing "Eurydice is back!"
(She was waiting for the Godblack Shine to arrive.)
A person is never in more distress than near the finish.
It's the same year when a spot of gin means warmth
for pinning papers on the cold street poles.
Not so long ago a body carried its own profile chart and rules.
A species of radio waves has replaced actual passengers
with a stillness even without birds.
Still the mystery of your life is that it's yours.
What are the indications? Rest and speech. Silhouettes of
beasts.
The pearls will roll, you'll see.

To Be Buried Where

I have forgotten most of my life but if I remember anything with the fullness of attention, I feel two things: that the original no longer exists and that she has been replaced by a paper reproduction. Anti-psychiatry, she forgets all her dreams in order to be free of interpretation.

For years you feel you are seventeen, way into your thirties and forties. Then you feel you are twenty-seven and then thirty-seven until you are in your late fifties. And then, almost overnight, you are a new species. "I left in your stars," someone said to me and I didn't know what stars she meant because I was thinning into an animal.

Yet the more this night of the sky becomes the case, the more I wonder if consciousness is outside our brains and bodies, if we are enclosed in a cocoon of mental zeal that dissipates or fades into "outer space."

Our skin absorbs culture and its hypocrisies as it navigates the earth and the weirdness of time. But it is a dreamy packet with golden strings dissolving into the other world.

When you are near to dying, you see hand-made patterns and textiles as if for the first time. You look closely at a scarf that you have worn for months casually, stroke and pluck it.

Now this little rag is a magnificent offering to the person that made it, intricate and uninterpreted.
An immortal structure underlies every piece of handiwork.

We are, in this sense, already in the other world. We stream into it. Or out of it?

The sun on water follows each person as a walking path. Wherever you step or stand, the back of the sun stays with you. To call into the sun with your eyes closed. Without a soul, to be afraid.

1630

Jean-Joseph Surin, a seeker-priest in France, wrote this:

"I found in the coach, placed very close to me, a young boy of eighteen or nineteen, simple and extremely crude of speech, totally unlettered, having spent his life serving a priest; but in all other respects filled with all manner of graces and such lofty inner gifts as I have never seen the like.

"He had never been instructed by anyone but God in the spiritual life, and yet he spoke to me about it with such sublimity and solidity that all I have read or heard is nothing compared to what he told me.

"When I first discovered this treasure, I separated myself from the group to be with him as much as I could, taking all my meals and conducting all my conversation with him. Apart from our discussions, he was continually in prayer, in which he was so sublime that his beginnings were ecstasies that were, according to him, imperfections from which our Lord had freed him. The fundamental traits of his soul are a great simplicity, humility, and purity. And thanks to his simplicity, I learned many wonders, however many others his humility may have hidden from me.

"I set him talking on all the points of the spiritual life I could think of for three days, as much in the area of practice as speculation, and I received answers that left me filled with astonishment. As soon as he became aware of what he was telling me, he wanted to throw himself down at my feet in humiliation, for we often alighted from the coach in order to be able to talk more comfortably and with less distraction. He thinks himself one of the world's worst sinners, and begged me to believe him.

"He spoke to me almost the entire morning on the various states of the most perfect union with God, of the communications of the three divine Persons with the soul, of the incomprehensible familiarity of God with pure souls, of the secrets God had allowed him to know concerning his attributes, and particularly his justice upon the souls who do not advance to perfection though they desire to do so, and the various orders of angels and saints. He told me, among other things, that he would not give up a single communication that God makes to him about himself in the course of communion for what the angels in the state of glory and all men might give him combined. He told me that a soul disposed in purity was so possessed by God that it kept all of its movements within his power, even those of the body, with the exception of certain little deviations in which the soul sinned. These are his own words.

"He told me that, to the extent that a soul was more in a hurry to attain perfection, it was necessary to do violence to oneself; that it was entirely the fault of the religious if they were not all perfect; people didn't persevere in conquering themselves; the greatest misfortune was that people did not bear up well under bodily suffering and infirmities, in which

God had great designs, and he unites with the soul through pain much more perfectly than by great delight; too great care for health is a great obstacle; true prayer consists not in receiving from God but giving to him, and after having received, giving back to him by love; when tranquility of soul and flaming love attains rapture, faithfulness of soul at that moment consists in divesting herself of all, as God approaches to fill her.

"I proposed all the difficulties of my inner self to him—by means of a third party, for otherwise I would have not been able to draw anything from him. In which he satisfied me in such a manner that I thought he was an angel, and that suspicion remained until he asked me, at Pontoise, for confession and communion: for the sacraments are not for angels.

"He never agreed to promise to pray to God for me but said he would do what he could; it didn't depend on him.

"I asked if he was devoted to Saint Joseph. He said he had been his protector for six years, that God himself had given him to that saint, without his consulting anyone. He also said Saint Joseph had been a man of great silence; in the house of our Lord, he spoke little, but our Lady even less and our Lord still less than either of them; his eyes taught him enough things without the Lord's speaking. In short, he told me such a great number of good thoughts that I am not equal to writing them down. And I am sure that those three days have been worth many years of my life.

"What I found particularly remarkable about this lad was an admirable wisdom and an extraordinary efficacity in his words. He told me the supernatural light that God pours into a soul lets it see all it should do more clearly than the sunlight shows sensible objects; and the multitude of things the soul discovers within is much greater than everything in corporeal nature; God in all his grandeur dwells and makes his presence felt in the heart that is pure, lowly, simple, and devoted.

"He told me of wonders for the consolation and direction of a soul that, attracted to prayer and desirous of virtue, is held back by physical infirmities; God requires of it a most angelic patience—after which, if it remained devoted, it would atone for everything in one hour. One of the loftiest discourses was how God works within souls through the Word, and the relations they must have to God through the Word in all of their dispositions, even in their sufferings.

"He told me the men of our profession who do not struggle against the pleasure of being praised by the world will never taste the joys of God; they are thieves; their darkness will ever increase; the slightest little trifle clouds the soul; what prevents the soul's freedom is a certain habitual dissimulation that holds it back. I use his own terms.

"I had to be very industrious, pretending to attribute no importance to him and persuading him that he was obligated by charity to converse with me by making some contribution on his part, since I couldn't talk all the time. And so he let himself go, and, being all ablaze with love, made no more objections but spoke on, following the impetuosity of his mind. As soon as I charged him to pray for me, he became less trusting and more on his guard. But being extremely simple and thinking himself the least of men, he revealed more of himself than he thought."

Wonders

Child trafficking is a form of modern-day slavery.
Traffickers target children who are vulnerable in some way,
promising them a better life, but then forcing them to live
and work in unfair, inhumane, or abusive conditions.
Traffickers use force, fraud or coercion in order to financially
benefit from selling another person.

Labor trafficking involves coercing someone into various
forms of labor, such as domestic servitude, factory or farm
labor, working in the hotel industry, begging, or other types
of forced labor.

Coercion may include:
False promises, threats, intimidation, debt bondage, holding
identity documents, withholding pay, using personal relation-
ships, deprivation of medical or dental care, lack of basic
necessities, threats including police or immigration, threats to
hurt family or friends, physical violence, and/or sexual abuse.

Rural children between the ages of eight and fourteen are
the most vulnerable.

Their parents may give them away under the illusion that

they are helping their children have a better life. Who could blame them?

*

Truth-telling and storytelling are crucial to children's survival of trauma.

Reports from UNICEF tell of children walking seventeen hours to be part of a tribunal testifying against people they knew who had committed acts of atrocity.

In Uganda a twelve-year-old commanded an army unit.

Children cry even when there is no one to hear them.

Memories forge future acts, for better or for worse.

If children find it safe to remember and report a painful event, they have a chance at recovering.

Often safety is not guaranteed to the truth-tellers because of revenge on the part of the people they name or their relatives.

This dilemma is where art/imagination/fiction comes in handy for the person speaking out. Coded language develops in cultures of poverty and oppression.

Children must be able to contribute to the solutions in post-conflict situations. They need to speak truth, coherently, and know that it is being recorded. Yet they need to be safe.

If their moral compass has been broken by drugs, they will need rehabilitation, but so will they need it for recovery from violence.

From the ages of twelve to twenty, a person's memories are most powerful and last through their lives. Before then, it is the unconscious that builds the child's life-character, events and people coming in at him or her, without borders or defenses against them.

*

Social norms among families and communities are essential to progress in human rights.
In the years between three and eight, the child learns what their rights are and what the social norms are in their nation-state.
Rights are not entitlements (I need a car), but the basic ingredients for growth (I need to read).

*

Slavery has been in this world since 6800 B.C. Modern slavery includes control through violence, economic exploitation, and the loss of free will. There are two hundred million slaves worldwide today.
Bonded labor, sexual servitude, and short-term disposable slaves (migrant)(organ trafficking)(cleaners)(children).

*

The adult world is split among those who exploit children (animals and the earth) and those who are organizing themselves to rescue them.

The children have stories of their own, desires of their own, and experiences that may not fit in with what either set of adults sees as "the truth."

Who is going to help the children tell their own stories?
We have to learn how to see the world through the eyes of children, but also to see where their sense of wonder (magic and miracles) can contribute to a vision of some-

thing new already here. This may be a fresh kind of realism given the unfolding discoveries of scientists about time and space.

*

The incidence of sexual abuse of children rises in refugee camps.

*

Enchantment produces a Secondary World into which both creator and spectator can enter together, trusting in the uncanny nature of the experience while they are inside it. Enchantment has its own logic and symbols, yet these refer to experiences we have very early. (People disappearing outdoors, returning, leaves falling, the wind blowing . . .)

On the other hand Magic produces, or tends to produce, an alteration in the Primary World . . . It is not an art but a technique; its desire is power in this world, domination of things and wills.
Magic and science share a long history. Look into alchemy.

The modernist project is analyzable in terms of interlocking domains: international capital, science and technology, and the nation-state. All of these depend on a single shared illusion among the populations.

In action, these forces are now inseparable; and Magic lies at their heart. Indeed, the power of modern Magic is such that via the media generally (and advertising in particular), the illusion has given rise to a new, third category: glamour.

Models, film stars, dolls and cartoons fall into this category. Plastic and bright colors. Without perceptions. They just receive our looks and do not pretend to be real. Glamour removes any possible chance of reciprocity, which is a huge relief.

The Ethics of Elfland

"The man of science says, 'Cut the stalk, and the apple will fall'; but he says it calmly, as if the one idea really led up to the other. The witch in the fairy tale says, 'Blow the horn, and the castle will fall'; but she does not say it as if it were something in which the effect obviously arose out of the cause. Doubtless she has given the advice to many champions, and seen many castles fall, but she does not muddle her head until it imagines a necessary connection between a horn and a falling tower. But the scientific men do muddle their heads, until they imagine a necessary mental connection between an apple leaving the tree and an apple reaching the ground . . . They feel that because one incomprehensible thing constantly follows another incomprehensible thing the two together somehow make up a comprehensible thing . . . The only words that ever satisfied me as describing nature are the terms used in the fairy books, 'charm,' 'spell,' 'enchantment.' They express the arbitrariness of the fact and its mystery."

Doctor, Doctor

I had my chance to give myself over to nature forever and lost it.
Now I have to die as a human in the hands of other humans, and I don't want to.

If all evil has its source in me, no wonder I live in the fear of God.
You say that the proof of sanity is the return to normalcy after a bout of wild behavior.
You say the success of a cure comes when the patient is freed from ecstasy as much as from despair.
But what if these are canals to a black source where silence is the depth of hearing?

You Doctor tell me to please get well and leave, but then you want me to suffer for you by demonstrating my ecstasies for your notebook.
You are the incarnation of benevolence in this hospital. Where would we women go otherwise—with our ennui, our inabilities, our fits?
The whole outside psychic terrain has been sprayed and sterilized against us.
You take care of us and keep us safe.

You are our Solomon but you live in a dry land. I know the warning: "Do not arouse, do not stir up love before its own time." But where will you be when the flowers appear on the earth and the time of pruning the vines has come, and the fig tree puts forth its figs?

Inside, at your desk? Staring at lazy women through a crack in the door?

You read the world physically but at a distance.

Sometimes you behave as if you are being persecuted by us your patients. I am treated as a "noble savage" because you sense that I am well educated, and there might be some male power behind me.

I love Bach, I read librettos, I play chess, I love poetry, yet you resist hearing my interpretations of my own problems because I don't use your jargon.

The Catholic Church gives as much significance to each act as any doctor does.

Traumatized by one day in history, generations have sat transfixed by the cross, unable to get to the other side of it, the resurrection, to forget what happened and move on.

It's a mass trauma that has lasted two thousand years, the crucifixion, and the children of this Church are of course riddled with psychoses and interpretations.

I understand Catholicism.

It's the only science I do understand.

The combination of thorough study with leaps of faith—well, this is the most reliable approach to the truth that I know.

So what you diagnose as narcissism is really just happiness. I am happy as a daughter of Jerusalem. It is my happiness that frightens everyone.

Sometimes in the midst of her story to the doctor, she would doodle, drawing diabolical penis-figures on paper bags.

The doctor looked at these pictures of little penis people living on the side of things, not on top, and assumed that it showed her vision of the world to be a wall, not a circle on which one stood, head up, but a vertical plane on which these creatures paraded like insects up and down.

She told him, from her point of view, that each figure was like a revolutionary who is just a common criminal who has concocted an ideology in order to justify a day's anti-social act. She used as an example the way that the doctor had arranged an entire hospital around his anxieties about evil women.

"Pathological thinking is overloaded with meaning. So who is the pathological one in this case? The patient or the doctor?

She added the obvious: "The absolute referent in the Western world is a white male adult intellect."
She said her neck was like a bottleneck, she would choke on her own words, and even quote Heidegger or someone, saying stuff about the excruciating experience of completing actions inside a vacuum.
Then she thrashed around the bed, legs spread, calling for Daddy or Catharine to come and take her home. He told her to cover herself and show some modesty.

Sometimes she would drop to her knees, rigid arms extended, and remain unmovable for hours. If he pushed down her arms, they sprang back into position again. Her knees grew red and sore on the floor, but she wore a serene expression.

For some reason the doctor couldn't even bite into his sandwich when she had spoken of her sex life.

His appetite was worse than nil. He felt revulsion for the whole world.

A thick exhaustion would follow and he would shove everything on his desk to the side.

She would penetrate him with her eyes, later, asking if he felt all right.

They faced each other through the window the size of an index card. She was often unwilling to see the whole of him.

He didn't indicate any interest in her question, but she always seemed to know anyway why he had failed to eat.

He was developing a theory from his "work" with her that the forgotten parts of a life are the very parts that give that life meaning, so that remembering them would actually cause harm.

Nonetheless he tried to get her to remember her childhood, but she always said: "I can't think of anything wrong. Only God knows what happened to make me like this. My sister is famous for her films about crazy people like me. My life is her material."

But one day she recounted an experience that she had had when she was very little.

Her mother had taken her into a store to choose the sweater she wanted for Christmas.

The store was like the interior of a lighted chandelier and smelled of sweet perfumes.

In the children's department she saw her sweater, it was navy blue with a parade of happy monkeys knitted across the chest.

On Christmas morning, when she undid the package, she found the wrong sweater inside. It was red. It had white diamonds knitted around the waist.

She didn't say anything but actually developed a fever and hid inside her bed, because in that one moment she realized that she would never get what she wanted in life. Not ever.

From her reference to the War he guessed she was in her late to mid-thirties.

She let him know that being herself was very painful as if she "were a mummy wrapped in painted canvas, and where the canvas meets the numb skin of my inner body, there is a terrible rubbing, a constant erasure of all possibility of remembrance."

He asked her why she walked in circles and she said she wanted to cast a spell on the ground, so that nothing could move forward in time.

"Only a ray of hope can thrive in this space."

He didn't give her electroshock therapy or strap her down on a bed in a straitjacket (the way he did with the other pajama girls) but put her tenderly in lock-up.

And again and again he tried to release her into the city, where she could either land in jail, or be returned to him, or die.

Since she could hold her breath without a gasp for well over a minute, and remain immobile for even longer, and since she could go without food, and did, for days, he believed that she could survive outside.

He suggested a religious life but she smelled his condescension, pinched her nostrils and waved at the air.

Then in order to encourage her, he pretended he believed in God and Nirvana—that they were the same—and because it was a time in American history when gurus abounded, he could refer to a system outside the psychiatric one as a possible method for curing her. She was grateful for his shift in vocabulary—from "psychiatrist" to "divine organ"—from "mania" to "ecstasy"—but wasn't fooled by his pretense at having faith in salvation.

It was nearly Christmas again, and she paced around the locked ward, where she had been placed after stealing meds from a nun who wrote JESUS on windows with her own feces.

She promised the doctor she would depart before the first of the year.

And on that eve she said she had a taste of blood in her mouth and it was the same as the bite of foil, or iron, making her teeth into shafts of pain.

On a chunk of wet apple strudel she saw whole cities as if through a metaphysical microscope.

She compared these cities to France on the eve of the Revolution, where bloodlust and madness consumed a whole population, and drove people to commit abnormal acts of torture in the name of an idea.

She identified the time she was witnessing as the Night of the Long Knives.

But the Berlin Wall was already up and dripping into the apples.

And she told the doctor that one of the Grimm brothers hoped that his fairy tales would simulate "the desire to wield a big knife, one that can cut through all barriers with complete freedom—at last."

The doctor pointed out that she was juxtaposing histori-
cal events and complained that he didn't understand the
recurrent metaphor of a knife, as if he were a critic and
she a poet.

Oblivious to his complaint she saw in the pastry the logi-
cal conclusion of all fairy tales: fat-cheeked girls plucking
eggs from the inside of living hens, flying knives cutting
off children's sucking thumbs, serpents with apples stuck in
their length, cooks with rolling pins slamming the heads of
geese, while ashes fell from the skies.

"Certain cultures love images of steam and snow sliced with
shining ice, and veils of fog shrouding islands on steel-gray
seas. They love gloom. They send others into exile in such
places with a perverse belief that it is a utopia the prisoners
are riding to—the utopia of absolute cold. They justify their
plans with this faith that they have in the absolution of mis-
ery, and that silver light that sheets the winterlands . . . "

She read all this on the sugary surface of the sopping strudel
and reported it to the doctor who assured her that the worst
had happened already. Not to worry.
"There is no future-laden world outside, then?" she asked.
You'll know about the future soon enough, he replied and
dodged her as she passed.

Franciscan

Poverty, writes Leonardo Boff, "is a way of being by which the individual lets things be what they are; one refuses to dominate them, subjugate them, and make them the objects of the will to power." The importance of this definition to a political artist in this century lies in its moral imperative. While you are enjoined to combat the outrage of poverty, you are also guided toward the values of a possessionless underclass. You literally save the poor, who in turn ensure a clear point of view toward reality, toward society. Poverty demands, Boff continues, "an immense asceticism of the renunciation of the instinct to power, to the dominion over things, and to the satisfaction of human desires." Poverty is, this way, not erased by the necessities (food and housing) but is, ideally, sustained by them.

The poor, by the way, means the earth and all the creatures that live upon it, the always-with-us.

The Pest

Georges Bernanos writes in his short novel *Mouchette* (1937):

"It had happened one holiday-time at Trémières. She was taking back to Dumont's café the fish which the old man had caught during the day—a basketful of eels. On the way a big fair-haired girl had bumped into her, and turned round and asked her her name. Mouchette had not answered and the girl had gently and absent-mindedly stroked her cheek. At first Mouchette had thought nothing of it, and indeed the memory had been painful until evening, and she had pushed it out of her mind. It had returned suddenly, changed and almost unrecognizable, just before dawn when she was asleep on the ragged mattress which Madame Dumont, on events when the café was full, put down for her in a narrow corridor littered with empty bottles and cans and smelling sharply of sour wine and heavily and greasily of paraffin. In some strange way, while she was half-asleep, she felt herself cushion her face in the crook of her arm and smell the imperceptible perfume of that warm hand, and indeed she seemed to feel the hand itself, so near and so real and living that without thinking she raised her head and put up her lips to be kissed."

Later Mouchette (a young teen) looks at her own swarthy calloused hand and is horrified. It is the sight of this hand that drives her into the blur of suicide. There is nothing in her drowning that is joyful or gives a feeling of spiritual liberation. Bernanos wrote: "The smell of the grave itself rose to her nostrils."

(Robert Bresson, who made a film from *Mouchette*, was preoccupied with teen suicide. In his first color film, *Une femme douce* (1969), the young woman, nearly a girl, kills herself. In *Le diable probablement* (1977) the boy wants to kill himself, and gets what he wants.)

Suicide is usually a reaction to an unlimited future. Rather than running and shedding the present in a state of blind hope, you falter and feel the whole weight coming at you. Suicide is the answer to one question; religion one answer to many questions. In the 1950s existentialism put suicide as the only logical outcome to a life of pure freedom.

Bernanos wrote: "People generally think that suicide is an act like any other, the last link in a chain of reflections, or at least of mental images, the conclusion of a supreme debate between the instinct to live and another, more mysterious instinct of renouncement and refusal. But it is not like that. Apart from certain abnormal exceptions, suicide is an inexplicable and frighteningly sudden event, rather like that kind of rapid chemical decomposition which currently-fashionable science can only explain with absurd or contradictory hypotheses."

One is seized by suicide as one is seized by love. The Devil prepares you for this grasp in small doses. Indifference, bad

luck, poverty, illness, verbal cruelty, changes of heart, betray-
al, slander: all of these are killers. Suicide is less common
during times of revolution because there is a surge of collec-
tive hope for a better future. Suicide is a surge of un-hope.
This is why it is more common to commit suicide when you
are abandoned by your lover than when you are widowed
by him.

Bernanos was harshly criticized: it is a scandal to simply
chart the miseries in a child's life that lead to her suicide.
Where is the lesson?

If suicide is seen to be a sin and the suicidal character is
the most sympathetic in the story, what is the moral judg-
ment being made? Is it possible that suicide is a movement
towards God? It can't be if God is indifferent, or if the char-
acter is indifferent to God. For both Bresson and Bernanos
the Devil is more forceful than God. Indeed, God's weak-
ness may be the source of all the trouble.

The moral burden is shoved away from God on to the ques-
tion of what a person needs to live in the world. (At least
one of three criteria has to be met for a person to survive:
one needs to be useful, to be loved, to be safe. Old people,
like the children of the poor, are often deprived of all three.)
This is what the story of Mouchette is out to discover. What
do we need in order to live.

The mystery of the story is that Mouchette loved the broken
Arsène and claimed him as her lover. In the movie, these
moments fly by almost too quickly. Mouchette is both
redeemed and made weak by the emergence of love in her
imagination. Her suicide is her way of ending her own story

before it is finished in the long human exhausting way. She ends it where it has found its meaning.

Her love for the maniac has a little history but it is essentially not chosen but delivered. It is automatic. *Au hasard*. She loves and cares for him at his most reduced moment, while he is frothing and twisting in a fit.

Bresson's Arsène is ugly, brutish, middle-aged. He shows no tenderness for the child whose hands wrap around his shoulders during the rape, and there is hesitation and deliberation in the girl's suicide at the end of the story.

Bernanos sees that she has been set up to die by experiencing love and that her consent to suicide is as natural as the man's epileptic fit. She just steps into the water.

Bresson who made films from stories by Dostoevsky as well as from Bernanos also confirms—through his nearly robotic models who serve as characters in his film—the belief of Simone Weil that necessity, gravity and labor are all of a piece. The imperceptible hesitation in each gesture in his films signifies gravity as a weight against which faith is in continual struggle. Just to take a step is an act of faith. You don't need to go further than that. The hand, the transaction. The step, the agreement.

"What is necessity without labor? Necessity must be regarded as being that which imposes conditions." This and other remarks from Weil's notebooks underlie Bresson's method. They also underlie the questions many artists and thinkers were concerned with after the Second World War. Suicide is the single act of freedom available to a person in the act

of becoming. In this case it was the Spanish Civil War that
gave Bernanos his story of a girl's undoing.

How Catholic is it? Its incarnational sensibility is what
makes it Catholic. That is, the forging of a soul takes place
on earth in time through suffering and pleasure, through
choice and degradation.

Simone Weil said: "If we behold ourselves at a particular
instant—the present instant, severed from the past and the
future—we are innocent. We cannot be at this instant any-
thing other than what we are; all progress implies a duration.
It forms part of the order of the world, at this instant, that
we should be such as we are. All problems come back to
the question of time." For instance, at any time a life can
seem complete enough.

Dear Bastard:

Now I can tell you that your little victim is only at home among nobodies, since she learned she was unloved. The gosling is warm within the wings of the mother goose.

There was a time when your mouth blew sweet messages into my ears, 'til I cried I'm safe, safe! But those were the hopes of another era, and they echoed in the air between us. An embarrassment, which you couldn't heal with more lies. You skirted this area, but we both knew it was there. On the right.

Indifference wounds; but deliberate cruelty can crush you. This is the sort of behavior that makes a person become excited by his or her stupidity, when he or she has done something right. That's the bruise you left on my other side.

Why you didn't let me participate in the ruin of our union, I'll never understand. This was something the managing classes do. Your sin against Divine precepts was, of course, far worse; but I won't name it, for fear of forgiving you.

Sometimes I wanted revenge. Then I wanted to track you down with my love. You're killing me with freedom, was my song.

One day, crushed by the disapproval of my fellow workers, I stood on an unfolding meadow which fell into a dark forest fulminating with secrecy, money and a violent history. I was dizzy from a desire to be understood, which was, more precisely, a desire to be *mis*understood. It was winter again, and the green needles were gleaming under thick leaves of snow. Why do you think you're so big, you asked, in a rush of face.

After pointing out the rudeness of the question, I was tempted to answer you with spit but made haste to smile. After all, I exist vaguely, half in one century, half in another, and as my points of reference disintegrate, others avoid me. This may be why I'm "too big." Lovers like addicts are too big to manage themselves.

Later, when you riddled this little palm with pinpricks, how different was my hand! No suffering is too big a price to pay for a sore palm. But my very weakness made me long for yet another storm of pain.

I went back to work pulling out the goose feathers for the rich man's pillow.

A no-win situation is "only human." When you want what you can't, ever, have, you can't not know this. No one's to blame if you can't face, or find, the absent facts. But what happens, then, is the same as when panic begins to accumulate with the inability to face the facts.

When you didn't answer my calls, I gave up wishing for us to be face to face, arm in arm. I wanted to be alone and androgynous, desensualized.

1. unpersuaded by sex or psychiatry
2. solitary
3. busy every minute
4. occupied half the time with philosophy; the other half with work
5. a service to others
6. soul-absorbed
7. so still, no one can see me
8. so fast, everyone wants me
9. a nurse to my patience
10. back in the nineteenth century

1922

Simone Weil wrote in her notebooks: "One must believe in the reality of time. Otherwise one is just dreaming. For years I have recognized this flaw in myself, the importance it represents, and yet I have done nothing to get rid of it. What excuse could I be able to offer? Hasn't it increased in me since the age of ten?"

To resist the reality of time is to resist leaving childhood behind. She called this resistance a flaw in herself, but is it? The self is not the soul, and it is the soul (coherence) that lives for nine years on earth in a potential state of liberty and harmony. Its openness to metamorphosis is usually sealed up during those early years until the self replaces the soul as the fist of survival.

She refused to buy the world on the terms it was offered to her (hammer of time, measure of value) because of the effects of a single childhood relationship. As a child, she struggled to survive losing to her brother and his phenomenal brain; and after the age of nine she began to construct an alternate set of conditions.

A few photos show her with him. He was three years older. They stood together dressed in white; he was wearing a sailor suit; they stood hand in hand, belly to belly, looking at the camera in 1911; then in another snapshot he sat in a little chair with his sandaled feet crossed while she leaned her head next to his. In 1916 they stood on a path with their legs uneven, she still leaned toward him and was dressed in white. And in 1922 they were seated at a table under some pine trees with books and big smiles. Here he was no longer a child and they look close in age. This was around the time she considered suicide, having realized that she could never achieve the learned heights of her brother, a scientific genius.

I see shadows when I remember these photos and white light dissolving on a path. She lives in the shadow of her brother, but she wears a crooked and charming expression for the camera. She is like someone who moves her body instead of the umbrella in order to get free of the rain and sun. From some accounts we have we learn that her brother struck her at times for her stupidity and then guiltily ordered her to strike him back. She obeyed and the striking sometimes turned into a fight until the parents intervened.

Like other siblings they read fairy tales together and learned how fixed a person's character is. Fate's kitchen is where the ingredients are dealt out. Temperament, body, social struc-ture—these would determine a whole set of future events and choices. A person performs a good or evil act only because she was fated to do so. The grotesque folk tales that revealed the potential of the civilized world to bake people in ovens and poison them with charm were just around the corner.

There were other stories too. Hafiz the poet wrote lines that would have pleased her as a child: "One day the sun admit-ted, I am just a shadow. I wish I could show you the infinite incandescence that has cast my brilliant image. I wish I could show you (when you are lonely or in darkness) the astonishing light of your own being."

Her brother became increasingly skeptical with the cocky assurance of the scientist he would become. Surely his point of view would prevail, impervious to doubt, in the mainstream of scientific imperialism.

His sister tried something else to control her inferiority. She made it into a good thing! She lost even more, but now deliberately. She chose the least-valued object between them; she made sure neither had more than the other unless it was he who had more. She found it unpleasant when her parents scolded him for something mean he did to her. She could not stand any acts of preference or the sight of someone being punished. This way she broke down the conventional posture of her self in relation to other selves, and preserved the transcendence of childhood instead.

As the years went by, and as many know, her brother became increasingly valued as a mathematician. He was a remote professor who, when asked, said of his sister and himself, "We saw each other only rarely, speaking to one another most often in a humorous vein." When editing her notebooks for publication, he removed her pages of mathematical equations that she had carefully scrawled there, because he was ashamed of her errors.

There is a strange power of resistance that takes hold of certain weak and incompetent people. They refuse to give up, despite a series of blows, errors and disappointments.

They annoy well-adjusted people because weakness is not meant to survive. There are many stories about weak children in folk and fairy tales and anyone can see that even if one of them has failed in the world, she still wants to live.

Tense and Raving

The present tense is the tense of emergency and ego. I don't like it telling a story. The past is the most convincing and carries a shadow on its back like a bag of stones. The past is always a little melancholy. Slate gray, sunless. The past is the best tense for storytelling. The storyteller drops the bag and sits down to look it over.

That there is a future tense is astounding. A night-thought soon to be abolished by daylight. See through it like water.

Which brings us to the subject of death. The underworld, the deep sea. No light ever.

The dead have taken off in search of deep time. They seem to have no feelings left for the living, or they refuse to tell the living what they really felt for them while they were all alive. This mystery is almost too much to bear for those left languishing on the top of the ground.

You must try to replace the dead who dropped you with someone else who will at least tell you how they feel about you before it's too late.

*

God hates me. I am someone who failed to be whole-hearted at loving others. I should have died for something by now. I know this is true but I hope that I'm asking too much of myself. I know that I'm a failure in this world. The only thing I have in common with God is that I don't exist.

Nobody sees my films because they are hand-made, home-made.

If they say God is love, I don't know what they mean by love, though I know what they mean by God. I have seen terrible things that a loving and powerful God, who was like a parent, would simply not allow to happen. I hate it when they give God attributes.
God is as plain as its meaningless name and a wafer.

To believe in something means to understand it. I wonder if the reason haters can be great artists and soldiers is that they put so much good into their work that the extra goes to making hell for everyone else. Why not do that, after all, if there is no Christ to be your best critic.

History is not a help, the way knocking wood is. Wood is a favorite of mine.

The dead are disgusting and the dead are divine.

They carry attributes for a while with them and then become slime and/or sky. I don't understand them. I don't believe in them. I hate them. They are often mean-spirited when they return, gluing their eyes to you. They whine about their problems with travel. Yet, in spite of this, I don't mind dying and joining them. Not that there is a choice. But the world and living can be at odds. Only religion, while I am alive, can span the two conditions. Ask God. The sanctuary is the space that opens into death as much as the hospital does.

The dead don't believe they are dead because a word like "dead" means non-existent and words only apply to what exists. That's why they don't understand what has been said when you use that word and they keep talking about being late and missing trains. One of them just looked at me from his youth unhappily as if to present his majesty in the role of tragedy. Never has one I knew returned radiant as in resurrected. Mary returns because she can't get over what the world did to her child. She is like one of those traumatized ghosts who still believe they are alive and completing a task.

She comes again and again, saying "This didn't happen!" holding her baby up. She carries that baby everywhere.

*

If they didn't know the whole story already, they would not know what tense to use. Most human stories end before death. The people die to life. But they had the past all wrapped up together in a book. They could have left it carved on a stone, but wanted to turn pages, to show how it feels to see things multiplying and speeding by very fast, then also being preserved and contained between covers. Words carved on top of a stone would not convey the way God is always in the present because God is always present so you can be confident of speaking of God as something that speeds past and gets lost simultaneously or vice versa. What is sad to discover is that events in this world are both pre-determined and whipped up at the moment they are occurring. People are bewildered by this paradox unless they can grasp the difference between time and timing. It is like the way they write out their calendar, make predictions and watch events unfold according to plan . . . And then it all goes wrong and a choice becomes necessary.

The choice seems to exist outside of the layout of time; there seem to be no precedents for what they have to decide. Has the result already happened? Is the choice going to affect all of history?

This is what is shocking about the story of Jesus whose life was prophesied down to its end and who nonetheless confused everyone when the prophecy was coming true. Peter had to make a big decision already knowing what the result of his decision would be. He failed three times anyway. He acted as if his life would be saved by remaining silent. This might have been the first time that determinism and free will came into slam-conflict, setting off earthquakes, an eclipse and a resurrection. Too confusing even for the heavens.

This must be why everything depends on how you place yourself in a book. The crucifixion is a kind of Christmas if the narrators already knew that he would be walking around on the next page. However, if they started with the resurrection, and left out his crucifixion, then you would not be sure he really died. Only having the resurrection directly follow the crucifixion proves that he died. I just wish it all could have begun with the resurrection and none of that suffering of mother and son had to happen at all.

Still, I better be glad that he really died because then I know something about one person that makes sense. You don't know that the others died because they never came back. Something else must have happened to make them stay away so long.

Jesus went into hell for three days and discovered death. He had to die of course in order to discover where the dead went and report back to us.

It was the discovery of the world. In the museum there is a picture of Jesus lying under a flat stone with a light on.

The material fact is that we are already in heaven, every minute inside the sky. No wonder the Vatican has a telescope!

Bewilderment

What I have been thinking about, because I can, is bewilderment as a way of entering the day as much as the work.

Bewilderment as a poetics and a politics.

I have developed this idea from living in the world and also through testing it out in my poems and through the characters in my fiction—women and children, and even the occasional man, who rushed backwards and forwards within an irreconcilable set of imperatives.

What sent them running was a double bind established in childhood, or a sudden confrontation with evil in the world— that is, in themselves—when they were older, yet unprepared.

These characters remained as uncertain in the end as they were in the beginning, though both author and reader could place them within a pattern of causalities.

In their story they were unable to handle the complexities of the world or the shock of making a difference. In fact, to make a difference was to be inherently compromised. From their author's point of view the shape and form of their stories were responses to events long past, maybe even forgotten.

Increasingly my stories joined my poems in their methods of sequencing and counting. Effects can never change what made them, but they can't stop trying to.

Like a scroll or comic book that shows the same exact character in multiple points or situations, the look of the daily world was governed only by which point you happened to be focused on at a particular time. Everything was occurring at once. So what if the globe is round? The manifest reality is flat.

There is a Muslim prayer that says, "Lord, increase my bewilderment," and this prayer belongs both to me and to the strange Whoever who goes under the name of "I" in my poems—and under multiple names in my fiction—where error, errancy, and bewilderment are the main forces that signal a story.

A signal does not necessarily mean that you want to be located or described. It can mean that you want to be known as Unlocatable and Hidden. This contradiction can drive the "I" in the lyrical poem into a series of techniques that are the reverse of the usual narrative movements around courage, discipline, conquest, and fame.

Instead, weakness, fluidity, concealment, and solitude assume their place in a kind of dream world, where the sleeping witness finally feels safe enough to lie down in mystery. These qualities are not the usual stuff of stories of initiation and success, but they may survive more than they are given credit for. They have the endurance of tramps who travel light, discarding acquisitions like water drops off a dog.

It is to the dream model that I return as a writer involved in the problem of sequencing events and thoughts—because in the weirdness of dreaming there is a dimension of plot, but a greater consciousness of randomness and uncertainty as the basic stock in which it is brewed.

Too clever a reading of a dream, too serious a closure given to its subject, the more disappointing the dream becomes in retrospect. If the dream's curious activities are subjected to an excess of interpretation, they are better forgotten. The same demystification can happen with the close reading of a text; sometimes a surface reading seems to bring you closer to the intention of the poem.

Sustaining a balance between the necessity associated with plot and the blindness associated with experience—in both poetry and fiction—is the trick for me. Dreams are constantly reassuring happenings that illuminate methods for pulling this off.

Recently I had this dream, which I will title *The Dream of Two Mothers*.

Two very old women—both of them mothers of actual friends named John and both of whom in real life have died—were in front of me simultaneously, and they were identical in appearance.

One represented the public (known) life, and the other the private (hidden) life. I knew this by their actions in the dream.

We were in a church basement and I said to someone beside me, "Enlightened yogis can see the aura trailing a person—it's a whole other version of the person, and sometimes I can see it too."

And as if to prove it, at that moment, someone all in red, even his flesh, drifted past us, splitting into sections, each one whole, as he moved.

His coloring was familiar to me because I knew about the red flush on the face of Moses and I had a feeling that Christ, reincarnated, was red too, and in many ikons there is a fiery red light surrounding the figures.

Red was the right color for this event and at the time I was even writing about it.

(In the dream, by then, I was conscious that I was in a dream and that I must pay attention.)

The man, now a priest, drifted upstairs with his multiple selves following to prepare for Mass, and I waited with the old women, where I had time to ponder the strange question of these two old mothers who in the dream were identical, though not at all so in life.

One woman might as well have been called Way Out There and the other one Way Inside, because one was rushing around doing things as a mediator, mother, Martha, and martyr for the other one who was still and pensive.

I could see, as increasingly nothing began to happen in the dream, that Way Inside could not exist without Way Out There—they were bound to the point that each was a different embodiment of the same actual human.

They were splitting and re-forming into one and the other, as birds can sometimes seem to do, whole flocks of the same shape bursting up into the sky.

And though it was not quite the end of the dream, these images at its center haunted me as if it had been a revelation.

While I can see that the Witness I (who perhaps could be called Q) in the dream expressed the bewilderment for which the Muslim of the prayer was praying for more of, the dream also illuminated a method for describing sequential persons, first and third.

As we all know, a dream hesitates, it doesn't grasp, it stands back, it jokes, it makes itself scared, it circles, and it fizzles. A dream often undermines the narratives of power and winning.
It is instead dazzled and horrified.
The dreamer is aware that only everything else but this tiny dream exists and in this way the dream itself is free to act without restraint.

A dream breaks into parts and contradicts its own will, even as it travels around and around.
For me, bewilderment is like a dream: one continually returning pause on a gyre and in both my stories and my poems it could be the shape of the spiral that imprints itself in my interior before anything emerges on paper.

For to the spiral-walker there is no plain path, no up and down, no inside or outside. But there are strange returns and recognitions and never a conclusion.
What goes in, goes out. Just as a well-known street or house forms a living and expressive face that looks back at you, so do all the weirdly familiar bends in the spiral.

*

The being both inside and outside simultaneously of the world is not just a writer's problem by any means.
To start the problem over again:
What I have recently noticed is that there is a field of faith that the faithful inhabit.

If you choose to enter this field after them, you enter questioning and you endlessly seek a way to explain and defend your choice to be there.

When you remain outside the field, you see that it requires no explanation or defense.

You, on the outside, perhaps better than those always inhabiting the field, know that it doesn't matter whether you are inside or outside the faith-field, because there is no inside or outside anyway under an undiscriminating sky. The atheist is no less an inquirer than a believer. In living at all, she is no less a believer than an unbeliever.

God's mercy can often seem too close to neutrality for comfort.

As Beckett has written in *Watt:* ". . . now the western sky was as the eastern, which was as the southern, which was as the northern."

Into such boundless perplexity King Midas—following his wish to have everything he touched turn to gold—wandered. Now he touched, but touched without receiving a response, only a hardening.

I remember that when I read this story as a child I already knew that there was a thin coating of gold on all objects. Whether the light was from the sun, or from an artificial bulb, there was always gold filtering over everything. So when I read about Midas touching his daughter, their roses, the water in the fountain, and the servants—and watching each one go solid—I felt that the potential had been there all along. It was frightening to realize that a simple wish could conjure up a surface reality and fix it to the roots. The lesson seemed to involve more than greed—it was about looking too hard and too possessively at living things.

The formation of his unhappiness lay in inhabiting an unresponsive world.

The hours he wandered through his gardens, among the leaden flowers, was he asking if he was really the author of all this? Can you wish a new world into being? And when he found that his child was a gold statue, while he remained free and sensitive, he must have been repulsed by his own hand. The usual interludes between fixed matter and a change in conditions were condensed into a spread of sameness.

He wouldn't ever again have to wonder: Where *is* the future?

He could now plan his future down to the smallest detail, which is really the definition of an anti-creation story.

In terms of bewilderment and poetics, the Midas story is a story that goes right to the heart of a purely materialist and skeptical position and shows the inherent error in it. The single-minded passion that drove Midas to wish that everything he touched would turn to gold ends with this question:

How could he survive on gold nuggets for supper?

Who would love him?

*

However I can't really talk about bewilderment as a poetics and an ethics without first recollecting the two fundamental and oppositional life-views that coexist in many of us. That is, the materialist-skeptical view and the invisible-faithful view.

Many of us know only too well the first one—we live it.

According to some Sufis, it was God's loneliness and desire to be known that set creation going. Unmanifest things, lacking names, remained unmanifest until the violence of God's sense of isolation sent the heavens into a spasm of procreating words that then became matter.

God was nowhere until it was present to itself as the embodied names of animals, minerals, and vegetables.

On the day of creation Divine transcendence was such an emotional force, energy coalesced into these forms and words.

Now the One who wanted to be known dwells in the hearts of humans who carry the pulse of the One's own wanting to be known by the ones who want in return to be known by it.

Lacking is in this case expressed by the presence of something—the longing to be loved—and so humanity, composed of this longing, misses the very quality that inhabits itself.

Ordinary problems of logic—like: Where were you before you got here? How did you arrive before my eyes?—foment in the background of this creation story.

Just as language evolves with increasing specificity, breaking further and further into qualifying parts, so words, as weak as birds, survive because they move collectively and restlessly, as if under siege.

This is at the root of the incarnational experience of being—that one is inhabited by the witness who is oneself and by that witness's creator simultaneously.

The question is, what is it to be familiar? (Why am I familiar to myself at all? Or is it my self that is familiar to some inhabitant behind my existence?)

The mystery of thought can only be solved by thought itself—which is what?

Martin Buber has written, "Every name is a step toward the consummate Name, as everything broken points to the unbroken." The awareness of both continuum and rupture occurring together may form the very rhythm of consciousness.

To the Sufis, words precede existence, perhaps because a cry brings people running.

Using a small grammatical ploy, the poet and philosopher Ibn Arabi reveals the overlap between the caller and the called when he writes that the Spirit wanted "to reveal, to it, through it, its mystery."

One "it" is not distinguished from another "it" by a capital I, or by quotes, or by calling "it" "itself"—as in "the Spirit wanted to reveal itself through its mystery."

Instead the sentence is deliberately constructed so that the Divine It and its "it" are indistinguishable and confusing.

In the Psalms the oscillation between You and He in one verse that refers only to the Lord in both cases may also be a syntactical method for dealing with simultaneity of a Way Out There and a Way Inside. But it is destabilizing.

In Sufi poetry, between the Divine seeing itself in the things of creation and sentient beings seeing the Divine in themselves, there is a constant oscillation and clearing and darkening.

Time is not a progression but something more warped and refractive.

Language, as we have it, fails to deal with confusion.

People fear repeating one word in the same sentence. They pause to avoid it every time, almost superstitiously.

There is for instance no way to express actions occurring simultaneously without repeating all the words twice or piling the letters on top of each other. The dream of coming on new grammatical structures, a new alphabet, even a new way of reading, goes on—almost as a way to create a new human. One who could fly and jump at the same moment.

But we don't even know if Paradise is behind or ahead of us.
    I can keep *un*saying what I have said, and amending it, but I can't escape the law of the words in a sentence that insists on tenses and words like "later" and "before."

So it is with this language problem that bewilderment begins to form, for me, more than an attitude—but an actual approach, a way—to settle with the unresolvable.
    In the dictionary, to bewilder is "to cause to lose one's sense of where one is."
    The wilderness as a metaphor is in this case not evocative enough because causing a complete failure in the magnet, the compass, the scale, the stars, and the movement of the rivers is more catastrophic than getting lost in the woods.
    Bewilderment is an enchantment that follows a complete collapse of reference and reconcilability.
    It breaks open the lock of dualism (*it's this or that*) and peers out into space (*not this, not that*).
    The old debate over beauty—between absolute and relative—is ruined by this experience of being completely lost! Between God and No-God, between Way Out There and Way Inside—while they are vacillating wildly, there is no fixed position.

The construction of high-hedged mazes is a concession to bewilderment, just as Robert Smithson's *Spiral Jetty* rises and sinks under the weight of Utah's salt water—both site and non-site—a shape that must turn back or drop off—that can climb and wind down—that has noetic as well as poetic attributes, miming infinity in its uncertain end.

The maze and the spiral have aesthetic value since they are constructed for others—places to learn about perplexity and loss of bearing.

And even if it is associated with childhood, madness, stupidity, and failure, even if it shows not only how to get lost but also how it feels not to return, bewilderment has a high status in several mystical traditions.

*

When someone is incapable of telling you the truth, when there is no certain way to go, when you are caught in a double bind, bewilderment—which, because of its root meaning will never lead you back to common sense, but will offer you a walk into a further wild place on "the threshold of love's sanctuary which lies above that of reason."

> *The summer's flower is to the summer sweet,*
> *Though to itself it only live and die . . .*
> — Shakespeare

This walk into the wilderness is full of falls and stumbles and pains. Strangely one tries to get in deeper and to get home at the same time. There is a sense of repetition and unfamiliarity being in collusion.

Each bruise on you is like the difference between a signature semiconsciously scrawled across a page and a forgery deliberately and systematically copied by a person who stops and watches her own hand producing shapes.

The forgery has more contour, more weight. In its effort to seem real, it cuts deeper into the paper and the fingers.

A liar can reproduce the feeling that a wilderness does.

In Sufism "the pupil of the eye" is the owner of each member of the body, even the heart, and each part becomes a tool under its lens. It is in and through and with the pupil of the eye that the catch locks between just-being and always-being. The less focused the gesture, the more true to the eye of the heart it is.

You are progressing at one level and becoming more lost at another.

*

The owner of the eye is the Divine Non-Existent about whom one can only speculate.

At certain points, wandering around lost produces the (perhaps false) impression that events approach you from ahead, that time is moving backwards onto you, and that the whole scenario is operating in reverse from the way it is ordinarily perceived.

You may have the impression that time is repeating with only slight variations, because here you are again!

Each movement forwards is actually a catching of what is coming at you, as if someone you are facing across a field has thrown a ball and stands watching you catch it.

Watching and catching combine as a forward action

that has come from ahead.
All intention then is reversed into attention.

Mentally, an effect precedes its cause because the whole event needs to unravel in order for it all to be interpreted.

The serial poem attempts to demonstrate this attention to what is cyclical, returning, but empty at its axis. To me, the serial poem is a spiral poem.

In this poetry circling can take form as sublimations, inversions, echolalia, digressions, glossolalia, and rhymes.

An aesthetic that organizes its subject around a set of interlocking symbols and metaphors describes a world that is fixed and fatally subject to itself alone.

Decorating and perfecting any subject can be a way of removing all stench of the real until it becomes an astral corpse.

*

In an itinerant and disposable work each event is greeted as an alternative, either the equivalent of respite or a way out.

Space may only indicate something else going on, somewhere else, all that lies beyond perceptions.

There is a new relationship to time and narrative, when the approach through events and observations is not sequential but dizzying and repetitive. The dance of the dervish is all about this experience.

> *Since the upright man is kin to the stumbling drunk*
> *to whose sultry glace should we give our heart? What*
> *is choice?*
> — Hafiz

The whirling that is central to bewilderment is the natural way for the lyric poet. A dissolving of particularities into one solid braid of sound is her inspiration.

Each poem is a different take on an idea, an experience, each poem is another day, another mood, another revelation, another conversation.

> *A void was made in Nature; all her bonds*
> *Crack'd; and I saw the flaring atom-streams*
> *And torrents of her myriad universe*
> *Running along the illimitable inane . . .*
> — Tennyson

What Shelley called "the One Spirit's plastic stress" and Hopkins called "instress" is this matching up of the outwardly observed and the internally heard.

A call and response to and from a stranger is implied.

Or a polishing of a looking glass where someone is looking in and out at the same time.

Particularities are crushed and compacted and redesigned to produce a new sound.

The new sound has muted the specific meanings of each word and a perplexing music follows.

Themes of pilgrimage, of an unrequited love, of wounding and seeking come up a lot in this tradition.

Every experience that is personal is simultaneously an experience that is supernatural.

How you love another person might be a reflection of your relationship to God or the world itself, not to the other person, not to any other person, mother, father, sister, brother. Untrusting? Suspicious? Jealous? Indifferent?

Abject? These feelings may be an indication of your larger existential position, hardly personal.

And the heart is an organ of the soul, in such a case, not the reverse.

In your cyclical movements you often have to separate from situations and people you love, and the more you love them the more difficult it is to allow anyone new to replace them.

This action can produce guilt, withdrawal, and rumination that some might read as depression. But to preserve, and return to a past you have voluntarily left— to suffer remorse—has always signaled a station in spiritual progress.

The human heart, transforming on a seventy-two-hour basis (the Muslim measurement of a day in relation to conversion of faith and conduct) in a state of bewilderment, doesn't want to answer questions so much as to lengthen the resonance of those questions.

Bewilderment circumnavigates, believing that at the center of errant or circular movement is the empty but ultimate referent.

> *Shall I compare thee to a summer's day?*
> *Thou art more lovely and more temperate.*
> *Rough winds do shake the darling buds of May,*
> *And summer's lease hath all too short a date.*
> — Shakespeare

For poets, the obliquity of a bewildered poetry is its own theme.

Q—the Quidam, the unknown one—or I, is turning in a circle and keeps passing herself on her way around, her former self, her later self, and the trace of this passage is marked by a rhyme, a coded message for "I have been here before, I will return."

The same sound splays the sound waves into a polyvalence, a rose. A bloom is not a parade.

A big error comes when you believe that a form, name or position in which the subject is viewed is the only way that the subject can be viewed. That is called "binding" and it leads directly to painful contradiction and clashes. It leads to war in the larger world.

No monolithic answers that are not soon disproved are allowed into a bewildered poetry or life.

According to a Kabbalistic rabbi, in the Messianic age people will no longer quarrel with others but only with themselves.

This is what poets are doing already.

"A thing of beauty is a joy forever," wrote Keats in the first line of *Endymion* and then hundreds of lines followed wrestling with the problems surrounding that grandiose statement.

The line, probably dictated to him in the Spicer sense, presented him with a hard subject, and he had to see if it carried through.

He circled it, pouring out sound-relations and image-associations that put it to the test of a true bewilderment, building an integrated system that turned, like the uroborus, back on itself.

The poem's last line is, "Peona went home through the gloomy wood in wonderment."

It is a very long lyrical poem. The stanzas are very long too.

Now we have lyrical poems that are written as fully wrought integrated units that include tiny stanzas and a lot of space.

One definition of the lyric might be that it is a method of searching for something that can't be found. It is an air that blows and buoys and settles. It says, "Not this, not this," instead of, "I have it."

Sequences of lyrical poems have the heave, thrill, murmur of the nomadic heart. Though they may at first look like static, fixed-place poems with a confessional personal base, they hold the narrator up as an idea, even an abstract example, of consciousness shifting in its spatial locations.

*

The same was true of early Celtic poetry that never went as high as myth, but never went as low as the purely personal, in describing the harrowing nature of pilgrimage.

As in Sufi poetry, in these short and long lyrical works there is a wide swing between experience and transcendence—the author is at one level empty of personality, a limited observer of their own isolation, and at another awake and interpreting.

> *The sealight where you float,*
> *The glint from lifting oars,*
> *Are also solid earth,*
> *Moulded yellow and blue.*

You see speckled salmon
Flash from the white sea's womb:
They are calves, fleecy lambs
Living in peace, not war.

These lines come from an eighth-century poem called "The Double Vision of Manannan."

The illuminati used flagellation, levitation, and starvation as methods of accounting for the power of the invisible world over their lives. Public suffering and scars gave the evidence of hidden miseries that had begun to require daylight and an audience.

The politics of bewilderment belongs only to those who have little or no access to an audience or a government. It involves circling the facts, seeing the problem from varying directions, showing the weaknesses from the bottom up, the conspiracies, the lies, the plans, the false rhetoric; the politics of bewilderment runs against myth, or fixing, binding, defending. It's a politics devoted to the little and the weak; it is grassroots in that it imitates the way grass bends and springs back when it is stepped on. It won't go away but will continue asking irritating questions to which it knows all the answers.

After all, the point of art—like war—is to show people that life is worth living by showing that it isn't.

Afterword by Chris Kraus

Maybe the sacred grove of our time is either the prison or the grave site of a massacre.
— Fanny Howe, *Indivisible*

"This book is made from torn parts," Fanny Howe writes on the first page of this short, devastating publication. Prompted (perhaps) by the United States government's spectacular cruelty towards immigrant children at the Mexican border, she assembles fragments of text she has written and read over the years that (perhaps) can catapult us towards an understanding of childhood and the paradoxical power of weakness.

These "torn parts" include fragments of two of Howe's novels, excerpts from her published essays, old teaching notes, and a poem by Ilona Karmel, who, along with her sister, was deported to forced labor at Buchenwald when both girls were still in their teens. The book also includes unpublished journal and diary entries, fragments of an essay by an American political prisoner, and the 1959 Declaration of the Rights of the Child adopted unanimously by the United Nations. Many of the people in Howe's fiction are spiritual and legal refugees of American twentieth-century radical politics. The pieces are held together by the strength of Howe's thought and a desire to understand where she's been as a person and writer. So, in a sense, this book is an autobiography via faith.

Still, I can't think of another contemporary writer who uses language as precisely as Fanny Howe. Therefore it seems best to take Howe at her word when she titles this book *Night Philosophy*. In it, Howe draws to the surface the essential concerns with social justice and activism, poetics and power, disappearance and God-ness, that have haunted her deeply poetic, formally radical, anti-capitalist work across decades, and actively questions them in spare, crystalline prose.

Living in southern California for fourteen years between 1985 and 2000 and teaching in San Diego, Howe has long been aware of the U.S.–Mexico border as a flash-point for economic and racial brutality. Felicity Dumas, the protagonist of Howe's 1993 novel *Saving History*, is caught in an impossible ethical bind, forced to transport illegally harvested organs from Mexico across the border in order to obtain a kidney for her own sick daughter. Tom, a radical lawyer she meets near the border, is considering joining a religious order because his failed defense of a political client resulted in a forty-year sentence. In El Centro, on the U.S. side of the border, Felicity tells Tom, "there are fake farms, a desert atmosphere, and a detention camp for illegals; the broad margin includes them as they wait for immigration papers. To the west, at night, helicopters flash down flood-lights and shoot into the underbrush; inside the helicopters are men whose people came to this country as immigrants."

"Catholic," one of the most powerfully aphoristic sections of *Night Philosophy*, was written during the years Howe lived in California. Waking at dawn to drive the hun-dred miles from her home in Hollywood to her job in San Diego, she captures the look and the smell of the dust and the sage and back alleys, the "lemon-water light of Califor-nia," and reflects on conceptual capitalism, the formation of character, and itinerant life. There is reciprocity between the material and spiritual world because "What you desire is what creates your quality. You are not made by yourself, but by the thing that you want." She wonders where she went wrong, she looks at the ugly nuclear plants and train tracks with lettuces wilting in boxcars: "It is imperative to find a virtue in itinerancy because this is the world now."

Howe famously converted to Catholicism in the 1970s, but she's Catholic in the same way the philosopher Simone Weil was Catholic, which is to say, she might just as easily be Sufi or Hindu. Howe's interests are in how the Catholic faith approaches language and ethics, ontology, solitude and community, and not in Church dogma. "The Church," she observed once, "has done tons of practical good for the poor, has managed to accept the maddest among us, and has a huge margin for visions."

"Limit, law, nihilism, failure becomes rage, remember the foul cruelty towards the weak child who cdn't speak English right, casual at my mercy, or cruelty," Howe wrote in a note to co-publisher Camilla Wills, a reminder of the aggression that drives her work to be maintained in the editing. Trauma, she writes here, can be survived through truth-telling and storytelling. And: "If children find it safe to remember and report a painful event, they have a chance at recovering."

In "Shut Up," a series of notes saved from a stay at a monastery on the cusp of the millennium, Howe interrogates her own recurring attraction to mysticism. Mere dialectics, recording experience, is not of interest. Rather, she's trying to reach something beyond experience, a disembodied presence she can only approach from multiple directions. "What was this strange preoccupation," she asks, "that seemed to have no motive, cause, or final goal and preceded all that writing that I did. Did it begin in the environment of childhood, or was it formed out of alien properties later?" For Howe, the purpose of literature is to transport both writer and reader into a heightened awareness of the invisible forces that shape our material lives. Childhood entails freedom from syntax: an openness that must be protected and can't be regained in a literal way.

The first pages of *Night Philosophy* recall scenes from a childhood that might be her own in a quiet apartment near Boston: a timeless lull interrupted by books whose pictures and words seemed to be shadowed by mysterious sources. Later the child, presumably grown into a girl, enters analysis with a benevolent doctor who praises his female patients at the asylum as anti-capitalists, "the last heretics against a work-addicted world," defending time against capital's instant equation to money. The girl puts the doctor to sleep with her stories.

But what, she goes on to ask, is a story? What is its purpose? In "Night Class for Children," Howe cleanly describes poetics as a unified structure that opens a door to the structure of life in the world. Fairy tales, legends and myths depict allegorical adventures through which the minor learns who to trust and how to read the subliminal signs of chance and coincidence. "The narrative structure reflects the way the storyteller reads the world: 1. as a social network with survival alone as its purpose; or 2. as a testing ground for a spiritual being who may or may not find happiness on earth."

Her 2000 novel *Indivisible*, a story told out loud to God, draws on her years in the 1960s and 70s as a single mother of three in a Boston neighborhood. Howe studies childhood not just to defend the rights of the child, but to show childhood itself as something like a poetic state of grace that must be advanced. Hers is a minor philosophy, in which the usual narrative movements around courage and conquest, discipline and fame, can be better replaced by the weakness, fluidity and concealment that marks a state of bewilderment. And these are the qualities that prove to be the most durable.

Howe's descriptions of injustice in *Night Philosophy* are harrowing because she lays them alongside her own heart. Boundaries are very porous. Further interrogating her own practice in "Dear Master:," Howe recalls her state of mind while writing poems, how she would "scrawl them all over the place as fast as I could, by hand, and then come back to the fragments and try to organize them as if they were spoken or a letter to someone and I knew what I was saying . . . Still, I have tried to recognize the missing figure behind the poem as it fled from one idea to another."

Working through the impeding bind of syntax to consciousness, to justice, to extremity, to trauma, to abandonment, *Night Philosophy* approaches complex, abstract questions by breaking them down to their most human level. Like Weil's *Gravity and Grace* and Walter Benjamin's *One-Way Street*, *Night Philosophy* is athletic. Howe coaxes the reader to enter a charged, active space where thoughts and sensations multiply and approach the invisible.

Sources

p. vii   "Seen no matter how...": Samuel Beckett, from *Ill Seen Ill Said*, published in 1982 by Calder Publications.

p. ix   "Lamb, you have fallen...": from a message inscribed in gold on a Greek tablet in the fourth century B.C. It was intended for the dead but was pulled from the wetlands in Greece when the waters shifted. Milk meant Paradise.

p. 2   "End-Song" is an excerpt from my novel *Nod*, collected in *Radical Love* by Nightboat Books in 2006.

p. 6   "A Useful Man": these notes on Jacques Lusseyran were gleaned from the story of his life, *And There Was Light*, translated by Elizabeth R. Cameron and published in 1963 by Little, Brown.

p. 13   "Night Class for Children": these are notes for an undergraduate class I taught at the University of California, San Diego and at Georgetown on the subject of childhood and writing for children.

p. 16   "1994": while in California, in the 90s, I corresponded and made friends with Marilyn Buck, a radical activist who was being held as a political prisoner outside Oakland. I met her a few times in the Dublin Federal penitentiary. She was known by poets and activists in the Bay Area who took her work and life seriously. Later she wrote an essay on self-censorship which Pasquale Verdicchio published in San Diego in 1995 as part of the Parentheses Writing Series.

p. 21   "The speed at which...": John Scotus Eriugena is quoted by Emmanuel Falque in *God, the Flesh, and the Other: From Irenaeus to Duns Scotus*, translated by William Christian Hackett and published by Northwestern University Press in 2014.

p. 24   "the habit of breaking open...": J.M. Coetzee in *Late Essays: 2006–2017*, published by Harvill Secker in 2017.

p. 24   "Human beings can carry...": from part seven of the 1801 poem "Bread and Wine" by Friedrich Hölderlin.

p. 25   "the true language of elsewhere": David Constantine in the introduction to *Hölderlin's Sophocles*, published in 2001 by Bloodaxe Books.

p. 26   "Childhood War" is the first half of a poem written by novelist
         Ilona Karmel in 1945 after three years spent in the labor camp,
         Buchenwald. She and her sister wrote during their imprisonment.
         Their poems were published in 1947 under the title *Śpiew za
         drutami* (*Song behind the Wire*) in a limited edition brought out by
         a Polish-Jewish daily newspaper called *Our Tribune*. The poems
         were handed to me by the Karmel family to find a way to translate
         them. It took seven years but in 2007 they were published by the
         University of California Press, translated by Arie A. Galles and
         Warren Niesluchowski, and adapted by me, under the title *A Wall
         of Two*.

p. 29   "The Plant": my description of the HASAG was written in
         2000 as part of the introduction to *A Wall of Two*. In the words of
         a Holocaust research paper: "The HASAG was an ammunition
         factory organized for the German war effort. The mechanization
         and automation of the production of small- and medium-size
         munitions enabled women to replace men in the assembly line.
         Women cost less than men. HASAG paid the SS less for women
         prisoners, both in the Reich and the *Generalgouvernement*. HASAG's
         experience with Jewish forced labor showed that, all other things
         being equal, women's adaptability and resilience were much
         greater than men's. The average mortality rate was higher for
         men than for women. Between twenty thousand and twenty-two
         thousand prisoners of different nationalities passed through the
         HASAG labor camps in Germany from their establishment until
         their final liquidation in April 1945."

p. 30   "We look at them…": their statement, "Letter to an Unknown
         Reader in 1947," was written as a preface to the poems by Henia
         Karmel, sister of Ilona, and later mailed to the Polish poet Julian
         Tuwim, whom they both admired. They never heard back.

p. 32   "The Rights of the Child" was composed at the United Nations
         in 1959.

p. 39   "Catholic" was written in southern California, where I lived and
         worked and drove a lot for fourteen years.

p. 54   "Tar Pits": La Brea Tar Pits are part of the Miracle Mile in Los
         Angeles. Excavations of bones from the Ice Age continue to be
         uncovered in the desert landscape. I lived astride them for one
         month in the 90s because the apartment I found was free for

the first month in that building and I could basically squat without furniture, light, or heat, but there was gas to boil water for tea. And then leave. Each day I walked with my dog up into the canyons. I wanted to be near the homeless.

p. 62　"1630": this portion of volume one of Michel de Certeau's *The Mystic Fable*—published in a translation by Michael B. Smith in 1992 by the University of Chicago Press—is taken from the chapter on Jean-Joseph Surin, a priest and seeker whom Certeau studied and admired.

p. 71　"The Ethics of Elfland": G.K. Chesterton wrote this passage in his book *Orthodoxy*, first published by Bodley Head in 1908.

p. 79　"Franciscan": *Saint Francis: A Model for Human Liberation* by Leonardo Boff, published in 1982 by Crossroad, in a translation by John W. Diercksmeier, is referenced in this piece.

p. 80　"The Pest": *mouchette* means "little fly" or "pest." This is a part of an essay I wrote as an introduction to the novel by Georges Bernanos called *Mouchette*, published by New York Review Books in 2005, in a translation by J.C. Whitehouse.

p. 83　"What is necessity...": from *The Notebooks of Simone Weil*, translated by Arthur Wills and published in 1956 by Routledge & Kegan Paul.

p. 84　"If we behold ourselves...": from *The Notebooks of Simone Weil*.

p. 88　"1922": Simone and André Weil, sister and brother, she a philosopher, he a mathematician, grew up together in France during the first half of the twentieth century.

p. 89　Hafiz was a Sufi poet and mystic in fourteenth-century Persia. His ecstatic poems have stayed fresh in multiple translations across the centuries.

p. 97　"Bewilderment" was first printed in my book *The Wedding Dress*, published in 2003 by the University of California Press.

Acknowledgments

I am very grateful to the presses who published the work in this volume originally. These include Sun & Moon Press, the University of California Press, Semiotext(e), Graywolf Press and Nightboat Books. My publishers and I would never have expected a book like this to emerge years later. This was thanks entirely to the adventurous Camilla Wills and Eleanor Ivory Weber and their meticulous scrutiny of the materials. The American poet, Oliver Strand, gave me invaluable assistance in arranging and editing them. Jacob Blandy did the final search for errors. The process was like star-gazing: staring into a night sky to locate a pattern. The brilliant and tireless Chris Kraus, in the end, was the one who would discover and assess that pattern. All the writers I refer to and quote from are people whose thoughts have accompanied my own over the years and my hope is that readers can find them as invaluable as I have.

About the Author

Fanny Howe is the author of more than twenty books of poetry and prose. She has taught literature and writing for many years. She is currently Professor Emerita in Literature at the University of California at San Diego. She has mentored a generation of American poets, activists and scholars working at the intersection of experimental and metaphysical forms of thinking.